Born on the First of Two

Anya Geist

Born on the First of Two

Anya Geist

Children's Art Foundation–Stone Soup Inc.
Santa Cruz, California

Children's Art Foundation–Stone Soup Inc.
126 Otis Street, Santa Cruz, CA 95060
www.stonesoup.com

Born on the First of Two
First published in the United States of America in 2021

ISBN: 978-0-89409-115-5 (hardcover)
ISBN: 978-0-89409-116-2 (e-book)

Library of Congress Control Number: 2021939344

Book design by Joe Ewart
Typeset in Quincy and Neue Haas Unica
Printed in the U.S.A.

Cover: *Enchanted*
(Canon SX600, Snapseed, Adobe Photoshop)

Sage Millen, 13
Vancouver, British Columbia, Canada

For
Matthew, Talia, Connor, and Greta.
You are the best cousins I could've ever asked for.

Prologue

*I*nhale, exhale. *Inhale, exhale.* The girl's breathing was labored and fast, the way it always was when she had this dream, this memory. It was a strange dream; it seemed to linger in her mind, tickling its edges like light in her peripheral vision. She'd had it for as long as she could remember, but she never became quite used to it; every time it came to her in her sleep, she found herself unsettled.

The sky was light blue, and the sun radiated its warmth down on the Earth. Birds chirped contentedly in verdant, leafy trees while bees hummed along as they flew from flower to flower, careful not to damage the soft, delicate petals.

The girl—then just a baby—sat on the ground just beyond the shadow of a small cottage, running her hands through the cool, glossy grass. She laughed at its touch, the way it slid along her chubby palm, and gazed up at the sky in wonder at the occasional fluffy cloud that drifted through on the mercy of the breeze, sweet air pumping its way into her lungs. She wanted to go up there. She wanted to be in that dazzling blue and run her hands along the clouds. She giggled merrily at this gorgeous day.

Here, the dream-memory became fragmented, shattered visions stabbing her mind.

The sky became dark, dominated by threatening clouds that seemed to reach up into space and cast jagged shadows over the June day. The birds stopped singing, and the temperature dropped.

She could feel the warm air leaving her lungs, cold, thick air forcing its way down her throat instead. It was searing, like a block of ice. She gasped for breath, rasping and wheezing, unable to cry as numbness spread through her, jamming into her arms and legs.

Two blurred figures appeared. One—she realized it was her mother—ran toward her, unclasped a golden necklace from her neck, and fastened it around the baby's neck. "You'll know how to find us," the woman whispered hoarsely.

The girl/baby, for now she was not sure which one she was, held out her hand, but her mother was already racing toward the gate in the white picket fence, rejoining her father.

"Stay back!" they called at the clouds. "Stop!" Their voices rang with fear and shook with weakness.

Now, outside the fence, there were many dark figures cloaked in dark robes that matched the army of clouds above. Their voices were deep and rumbling, like thunder that was mad, thunder on a rampage.

"No!" the girl's parents shouted. "Stay away!" But the figures were advancing, opening the gate, and the coldness was tightening its grip and the wind was howling.

Then her father turned to the sky, tears in his eyes. "Save her!" he yelled. His voice echoed into the sky.

And suddenly the air twisted like vines wrapping around a tree, and the girl was falling up, sucked into a dark tunnel. The coldness vanished, replaced instead by a constricting feeling as the air and darkness seemed to tighten—for it was as if they were one thing—and the girl was left writhing, shouting into emptiness as she tried to fall back to Earth to see her parents one last time.

She awoke. Her sheets were twisted and her chest tight, as if there were cords binding it. She sat up in bed, panting, and clutched her neck, grabbing the golden necklace that had been placed on her so many years ago. She wrapped her fist around it, feeling the cool metal soak into her sweaty hand, and tried to relax, staring into the rich darkness of her room, so different from that of the tunnel. She knew it would be a long time before she allowed the waves of sleep to crash over her once again.

Part One

CHAPTER 1

Stars Up and Down

"Maya!" Auntie's voice flowed like honey, rich and deep, through the little house.

"What?" By contrast, Maya's voice was sharp and clear, like water.

"It's suppertime." Auntie stood at the foot of the stairs, shouting up to her niece's room.

"But I'm busy, Auntie," Maya complained. Auntie could hear her sigh.

"Maya, in the eleven years you have lived in this house, you have never once skipped supper, and I do not intend for you to start now." Auntie's tone should have told Maya that this was nonnegotiable.

However, Maya either didn't pick up on this, or ignored it. "But I have homework!"

"You can do your homework after supper!"

In her room, sitting on her bed, Maya jutted out her jaw. "Do I have to?"

"Yes. Now I'll be out on the porch. Get your supper and come out there." Auntie's receding footsteps told Maya she was going outside.

Begrudgingly, Maya slid off her bed, lay on the floor for a good ten seconds just out of spite, then picked herself up and began storming down the hallway and downstairs. She wasn't *mad*, per se, just highly annoyed. However, it is always more fun to storm downstairs than to walk.

She picked up a plate of spaghetti in the kitchen and headed out onto the porch, sitting down with the air of someone who is being forced to do so. "Are you happy now?" She glared at Auntie.

Auntie sighed placidly and swirled her spaghetti around with her fork. "Maya, I'm always happy when you're with me."

Maya's hard, emerald-green eyes, flecked with silver and gold, softened for a moment before she resumed her pretense of anger. "Hmph." She stabbed a meatball on top of her spaghetti. Her thoughts blew around crazily as she tried to find a way to fuel the fire of her own annoyance. As she settled on the perfect method, her eyes lit up slightly, the green becoming more alive, a wild forest.

Before she had a chance to speak, though, Auntie interjected: "Maya, why are you avoiding my eyes?"

"I'm not," Maya answered, all too guiltily, her eyes wandering to a spot just over Auntie's ear. "You know," she began, preparing to launch her dagger of anger into Auntie's heart, "my p—"

"Maya." Auntie's voice was firm now, not concerned, but curious. "Why aren't you looking at me?"

Instead of answering this time, Maya just went ahead and launched her attack. "My *parents* would have let me do my homework and miss supper." Her voice was laced with poison.

Auntie did not look provoked, though. She merely shook her head sadly. "Maya, don't go there. It's not fair."

"Not fair to *you*, maybe," Maya exclaimed, now truly angry without knowing why. "Because you know I'm right!"

"No—" Auntie tried to say, her blue eyes swimming.

"Have you ever thought that maybe it's hard for me to not have parents, huh? Have you ever thought that it's weird living with someone I call my aunt, someone I'm not even related to?" Darkness was setting around them, though the porch remained illuminated. The stars were beginning to come out, and the night air was cool and sweet.

Maya's eyes shone with tears, but still she avoided Auntie's gaze. She fingered the golden necklace around her neck. A thin pendant hung from the chain, and as Maya traced her fingers over the engraving of a dove, it grew warm to her touch.

"Maya," Auntie pleaded. "Look at me."

"No."

"Maya, please. You don't want this anger. It doesn't deserve you. You are better than it."

"I—"

"We both know that you get caught up in your anger very quickly. But you don't have to. Look at me."

"I don't want you to use your power," Maya spat out. They both knew what that meant. Auntie's power was to calm people down, the way others could teleport or fly.

Maya hated the way it felt when Auntie used her power, the way it seemed to submerge her in a garden of sweet-smelling flowers. The way it forced the anger out of her, whether she wanted to keep it or not. It didn't matter whether her anger was justified or not—Maya wanted to be the one to send it away, not to have it overpowered by perfume.

Auntie stared at the table. "Okay. You need to calm down, though."

"I know," Maya admitted. She could feel her anger slipping away from her, vanishing through the cracks in the porch.

"Look." Auntie tilted her head. "Look out past the porch. The night is so beautiful. The stars are too." Her face adopted a serene glaze as she looked off into the darkness.

"The stars are always beautiful," Maya muttered, her anger rallying one last time. Still, she stood up, her chair scraping the wooden porch, and rested her elbows on the porch railing. The wind swept her dark brown hair over her shoulder, stroking it like a parent she couldn't have.

"I wonder what it's like down on Earth," she mused. "I wonder if they look up at the clouds and wish they could be up here with us." She recalled having had that very thought in her dream. How strange it was that she had been brought up to the Land of the Clouds immediately after desiring that very thing.

Auntie came to stand with Maya. Together they looked out into the darkness, at other homes, at the towns of the Land perched delicately on the tops of clouds. "It's beautiful there," Auntie sighed, recalling her adventures on Earth. She looked down, where a gap in the clouds revealed tiny orange lights—human life. There were stars up and down.

"Though not many people ever get to see it."

Maya kept her mouth firmly shut, knowing that this last sentence was directed at her, a sort of "don't even think about it until you're old enough." In her mind, however, she was already travelling to Earth. What would it be like to see the stars from down there?

CHAPTER 2

The OCT

The next morning dawned bright and clear. The sun had just come up when Maya awoke to her alarm. She turned it off and rose from bed, shaking sleep from her eyes. Pink-golden light spilled into her room, coating her desk and bureau, bed and bookshelf. She pushed the window open and let the sunlight hit her face, relishing its warmth in the frigid morning air.

She dressed in a simple tunic and cloak, then proceeded to go downstairs for breakfast. The smell of scrambled eggs caused her stomach to grumble. Auntie was setting two pieces of toast on plates, her silver hair neatly plaited, as Maya sat down at the kitchen table. As there was no precipitation above the clouds, they ate supper on the porch almost every evening, after the sun had warmed the wooden floor. But in the morning, it was still too cold to sit outside.

"Good morning," Auntie said. Her tone was welcoming and warm, like an embrace, but Maya sensed a note of hesitancy. Neither of them had forgotten their fight from the night before.

"Morning," Maya replied, greedily grabbing a plate of toast and nearly shoving it down her throat. It crunched pleasantly in her mouth. "Where are we today?" Maya inquired through a mouthful of toast.

This was not an odd question in the least. In fact, most children asked it every morning and evening as well. Since the "land" of the Land was clouds, they often moved from place to place—wherever the wind blew them—every day.

It was an exciting game for little children who loved trying to guess the correct answer, and an interesting bit of trivia for everyone else.

"We're over southern France this morning," Auntie informed Maya. "So it should be warmer today."

"Good," Maya said. She supposed weather could be cold on Earth, but it could be absolutely freezing in the Land—frigid to the point where you had to wear three heavy layers.

Maya finished her breakfast and bid farewell to Auntie as she grabbed her backpack and headed out the door, wrapping her cloak around herself.

She skipped along the sidewalk, careful to stay away from the precipice at the edge of the cloud. People did occasionally fall off. Some could fly back up. Maya had no idea what happened to the others.

"Hey!" a voice called from near Maya. She whirled around and saw her friend, Scarlett Clayden, leaving her house, her two little sisters in tow.

"Hi, Scarlett," Maya yelled back, walking toward her friend. "What's up?"

"Nothing, really. I have to take my sisters to daycare this morning because Mom's on an assignment."

"Oooh." Maya's eyes sparkled in the sunlight.

"Yeah. I don't know much about it, but if you wait for me in the park while I drop these two off, we can walk to school together and I'll tell you."

"Sounds good. See you there." Maya started off again. As she left her neighborhood, with all of its houses in neat rows, she began to see more and more people. Some biked in the streets, some walked, and some flew. And Maya knew there were many more commuters who were teleporting.

She reached the park, with its towering trees, and sat down on a bench. The ways of the Land were unknown to most people. In school, they learned about Earth and its people, but they never really talked about why the Land worked the way it did. As far as Maya was concerned, no one knew how trees could grow above the clouds, or how the citizens of the Land could survive, and even thrive, in cold temperatures that could kill a human. The Land of the Clouds was a mystery, and Maya was fine with that.

She was just pulling out some homework about the geography of Earth when Scarlett strode up to her. "Hello," Maya said, looking up at her friend.

"Hey." Scarlett sat down on the bench next to Maya and peered over at the homework Maya had out. "It's 'plateau': P-L-A-T-E-A-U, not 'plato.'"

"Oh, right." Maya grinned sheepishly. "Wait, what did you get for question four? 'Liquid precipitation on Earth?'"

"Rain."

"Okay, same." She stood, and they began to walk. "So, the assignment?"

The two girls were obsessed with Scarlett's mother's assignments. She was part of a select group allowed to visit Earth in order to make sure that the world was running smoothly, that no human was in danger of messing it all up. Maya and Scarlett got up from the bench and walked through the lovely green park as Scarlett told Maya all that she knew.

"Mom didn't say much. But, you know, she never does about these things. I suppose they're probably top secret."

"Top secret," Maya sighed pleasantly. "I would *love* to be a part of a top-secret mission."

"Yeah," Scarlett agreed, nodding so that her long platinum blonde hair swayed slightly. "Anyway, she said it wasn't a very big mission. There are only two of them going down to Earth this time."

"When's the mission?" Maya asked. Like "where,"

"when" was not a terribly uncommon question. The Land of the Clouds existed outside the flow of time. It was like a fern on the bank of a large river. Though the fern might get splashed by water sometimes, it wasn't a part of the river.

"Um . . ." Scarlett scratched her chin in thought. "I think my mom said 1400s CE. Whenever there were all those kings in Europe."

Maya sighed again as they passed a small office building. "I would love to time travel."

"We're learning how to in school. In just a few years—"

"I know, I know. But I'm ready now. I want to time travel. I know I could time travel." Her voice was yearning, betraying her obsessiveness. Her eyes glittered frighteningly.

"Maya," started Scarlett, raising her shield, preparing for an argument.

"Don't 'Maya' me! I'm ready!" Maya could feel the heat in her tone rising. "I'm the best in the class, and I want to get out of here!"

She began walking faster, leaving Scarlett in her wake. It was true. She knew she was the best in the class at the principles of time travel. So why wouldn't anyone let her do it? *It isn't fair*, she thought, practically screaming the words in her head.

Maya's cheeks were flushed with anger by the time she reached school. She wrenched open the door to her classroom, stomped to the back of the room, and sat down in her seat. Scarlett came in a few minutes later. She stared at Maya for a moment as if trying to read her mind, then took her own seat two rows away.

At 7:15, the bell rang for first period. It wasn't loud, just a faint buzz in the background.

The teacher, Sir Galiston, entered the room, sweeping his cloak as he did so. Tall and broad, he looked like a hero from one of Earth's medieval stories. Amused by Sir Galiston's entrance, Maya almost turned to roll her eyes at Scarlett before remembering that Scarlett was probably still mad at her.

"Good morning, class," Sir Galiston said. His voice was high pitched and squeaky, like that of a baby bird.

"Good morning, sir," responded the class in a dull fashion. Their lack of enthusiasm wasn't due to the fact that Sir Galiston's class was *bad*. More that he was often overdramatic. In fact, Sir Galiston was one of the best, most experienced teachers in all of the Land, having been on the front lines in one of the greatest battles of all time. He would regale them with stories most every day in his class, History of the Land. Today was no exception.

"Now," he announced in his strange chirp. "The next subject in your curriculum is the War of the OCT. Luckily for you, I fought in that war." He made a flourished bow, and half of the class, Maya included, smothered their giggles.

It was hard for Maya to stay angry and on edge when Sir Galiston told stories. He made them bright and fun, unlike the textbooks, which turned lively tales into dry dust. And as Sir Galiston began, Maya felt her anger receding like the tide. It was not gone, just removed from her focus for the time being.

"It must have been over a hundred years ago," Sir Galiston said, striding up and down the front of the room. "I was only a boy—well, I was seventeen. I had just discovered my power . . . Yes, seventeen," he repeated, seeing their looks of astonishment. "It was much more common to discover your power around age sixteen or so back then, not at twelve.

"Anyway, my power, as I'm sure you all know, is flight. Not a terribly uncommon power, but still . . . Now, who here actually knows what the OCT were?" Only a few students raised their hands, Scarlett among them. Maya supposed her mother had told her about them.

"Ah, well," mused Sir Galiston. "I should probably tell you about them, then. 'OCT' stands for the Organization to Control Time, and the Octagons were People of the Land of the Clouds, just like you. You kids all know how we try to interfere with human affairs as little as possible, right? Well, the OCT wanted to control time and the outcome of human events. That completely violated the Standard of Time Travel, which stated that we would use time travel only to keep humanity safe.

"They wore awful black robes with an octagon emblazoned on the back and always traveled in groups of eight. It was their lucky number." Some giggled, most likely at the notion that an evil organization could have a lucky number.

"No—don't laugh. The Octagons were dreadful people. Their motto was 'Beware the storm,'" Sir Galiston continued.

"Anyway, there were several skirmishes between them and the rest of us in the Land before the great battles began. Their leader, Fredrick von Hopsburg, had the power to transform his appearance and often appeared as a young boy. One skirmish began when he . . ."

And so Sir Galiston rambled on, describing the war in enthralling detail and also recounting his own brave actions that saved the mayor, leader of the Land. "Thus," he concluded, "we good People of the Land vanquished the OCT. However, I must tell you, they are still out there. They mostly reside on Earth now, hiding in the shadows, making mischief, interfering with human governments and history. Many of the Land's missions to Earth involve correcting their mistakes."

Maya saw many of her classmates cast a furtive

glance at Scarlett, whose cheeks were now turning cherry red; the class knew about Scarlett's mother.

"There will undoubtedly be a time when the OCT attempts to regain its former might," Sir Galiston informed his pupils. "As you should know, after the war, Grenna the Great made the prophecy that is now engraved on the fountain in every town square across the Land of the Clouds."

Many students nodded at this. Most of them, Maya included, walked past the fountain every day.

"The prophecy goes, 'The child—'"

But at this point, the bell had hummed and Sir Galiston dismissed the class, shouting after them in his squeaky voice that he would carry on with this story tomorrow.

CHAPTER 3

Chosen

At 2:30, when the sun was high in the clear blue sky and the air was warm enough that the People of the Land were shedding their cloaks and letting sunlight pour onto their faces, the end-of-day bell rang.

Maya and Scarlett met on the sunbaked school steps, their bags heavy with homework. They began walking in silence, neither able to start a conversation. Maya looked around at the buildings as they walked into the city and toward the park.

They crossed a cobbled street, narrowly avoiding an accident with a bicycle—for there were no cars in the Land—and were walking in front of a tall, grey, shining building that reflected the sunlight in a subdued way, almost as if it were absorbing some of the light. "This is it," Scarlett announced abruptly, stopping in her tracks and staring at the building.

Maya's stomach coiled into a knot. *This is it?* What did she mean? The anger in Maya's stomach began to rumble, getting ready to charge. "What?" she asked. Her voice sounded as if it had been stretched. "What is it? This is just the government building, Scarlett."

"The prophecy."

This statement shocked the anger back into the pit of Maya's stomach. What did she mean "the prophecy"?

The confusion must have shown on Maya's face, for Scarlett stared at her slight friend, eyebrows raised.

"Oh!" Maya exclaimed. She berated herself for being so stupid. *The prophecy.* The prophecy that was engraved in every town square in the Land, as Sir Galiston had reminded them. Maya turned. Across the street from the government building stood a great fountain, hewn from pearly stone and spouting clear, tinkling water into a shallow pool.

"Let's go look," Scarlett said. She began crossing the street.

"Oh, yeah. Right." Maya followed her, her mind a blur. Was it possible that Scarlett was not mad at her for her outburst that morning, that Maya had been imagining the mountain of tension between them?

The two girls stood in front of the fountain. Four lines of slanted writing shone at the bottom of the pool, light rippling across them and making them seem magical. Although Maya had passed here before, had read these lines, she was still in awe as she soaked them in.

> *The child born on the first of two*
> *Who knows it is their fate*
> *Shall harness powers most impressive*
> *To defeat the enemies of eight.*

"What do you think it means?" Maya wondered.

"I'm not sure," mused Scarlett. "I mean, everyone knows the last line refers to the OCT."

"Yeah . . ." Maya was thinking. The men in her dream, in her memory, the ones who came to the front gate on that beautiful-turned-dark June day—they had been wearing dark robes. Could they have been Octagons? After all, they had been on Earth . . .

The girls started walking again. They didn't talk for a few minutes, but this time because they were both deep in thought. Maya considered the prophecy again. "The child born on the first of two." Her own birthday was February 1.

February 1. The second month. The first day. 2/1. First day of month two. Maya froze. She stood so still she might have been a statue. She barely dared to breathe.

Scarlett turned and looked at her, concern etched on her face. "Are you okay?" When Maya proceeded only to take more tiny breaths, Scarlett's brows furrowed deeply. She shook her friend. "Maya? Maya?"

Maya forced herself to take a deep breath. "I'm okay." She could hardly summon more than a whisper.

"What's the matter?" Scarlett bent down to look Maya in the eye.

"It's nothing." Maya felt like her eyes were spinning, the flecks of silver and gold going round and round and round. She swayed dizzily.

"It's not nothing. Tell me what's the matter."

Maya took another deep breath. "You're not going to believe me."

Scarlett crossed her arms. "Try me."

"My birthday," said Maya in a conspiratorial whisper, fully aware that she sounded like a raving lunatic, "is February 1."

"So?" Scarlett looked untroubled. Maya gaped at her.

"So? February 1. Think. The first day of the second month. The first of two."

Scarlett's hazel eyes widened significantly. "No, no. There's no way. No. No, no, no. Are you sure you're okay? Have you been drinking enough water?"

"I'm not crazy, Scarlett!" Maya protested.

Scarlett raised an eyebrow. "Really? Because you sound crazy. Normal people don't just decide they are the subject of a famous prophecy. And don't you dare say you aren't normal," she added, pointing an accusatory finger at Maya.

"No, I'm right!" Without thinking about it, Maya

fingered her necklace, bringing it out from beneath her tunic.

"So that's what this is about? The necklace?"

Maya glared at her, and Scarlett raised her hands placatingly. "Sorry, sorry. I know your parents gave it to you." She sounded sincere. "But that doesn't mean—"

"But what if it does? Why were my parents attacked? Who attacked them?" Maya could feel her voice rising, the dormant anger in her stomach being swallowed by a hunger to be something great.

Scarlett eyed her suspiciously, as if trying to read her mind.

"You can't read my mind," Maya informed her, quite unnecessarily. "Your power—"

"I know what my power can and cannot do," replied Scarlett dismissively. Scarlett had found her power young, at age ten, Maya recalled with a surge of jealousy. By merely touching an object, she could tell its history, perhaps even glimpse its future. It was an ability few had (even fewer nowadays, as a matter of fact), and whenever Scarlett used it, Maya was reminded that she had not discovered her own power yet.

"Aha!" said Scarlett triumphantly.

Maya was shocked. She stared at Scarlett. "What?"

"Maya," Scarlett began in a knowing, perhaps condescending, tone. "What day is it?"

"June 9." Maya was oblivious as to why this mattered, and then it hit her. She didn't stagger, more crumpled a little bit.

"See?" Scarlett told her.

"I didn't even realize!" Maya exclaimed. June 10 was the day she had been pulled from Earth up into the Land of the Clouds.

"You always get like this around the anniversary,"

Scarlett reminded her as they started walking again. "Like you need to prove yourself."

"But I'm right." Maya was playing with her necklace again, pulling the chain taut and pushing her chin into her chest so she could scrutinize its every detail.

Scarlett sighed, perhaps sensing that this was a battle she was not going to win. "Can we talk about something else?" she asked.

"Fine by me."

And so they passed the rest of the walk home with mindless conversation about school, the weather, anything that didn't relate to the prophecy. Scarlett tried to put the thing out of her mind, sure that Maya would forget about it in another week, once the anniversary had passed. But Maya was thinking as hard as she could about it: could she be the child in the prophecy?

When the girls reached Scarlett's house, Scarlett turned to walk down her front path, but Maya stopped her. "First, hear me out, please."

Scarlett looked like she was trying very hard not to roll her eyes, refraining from doing so only in the interest of preserving their friendship, which was quite a nice thing when Maya wasn't going off on tangents about things like time travel and prophecies.

"Listen. It all makes sense," Maya was saying. "There has to be a reason why I was taken from Earth, a reason why my parents were targeted. The prophecy fits, and look at my necklace. There's an address on the back. I bet that's where I need to go. Besides, there's got to be a reason why I'm so good at the concept of time travel, and why I'm so eager to do it, and why I've always wanted to go to Earth." To Maya, it fit smoothly, each piece of the puzzle clicking into place.

Scarlett sighed. "Maya. Please be reasonable. You

know we can't time travel yet. Our teachers have told us—told you specifically—that it simply requires too much concentration. You could die."

"I'm not waiting until I'm sixteen if I'm supposed to save the world!"

"But what if you're not?"

"Scarlett, please! You have two great parents. You don't have to wonder what happened to them or why you had to leave them. I don't even remember anything about mine, except for that dream I have, and that's a nightmare!"

Scarlett opened her mouth, then closed it, biting her lip. "If you think you're the chosen one . . . I'll see you in the morning, Maya."

And with that she turned her back on her friend and headed up the front path, leaving Maya to finish her walk home alone.

CHAPTER 4

Vanish

Maya returned home that afternoon deep in thought. She didn't care what Scarlett said—she was convinced that the prophecy related to her. She hurried past Auntie, ignoring her call of "Good afternoon! How was school?" and disappeared into her bedroom.

This was not an uncommon occurrence, because Maya often had homework and tried to do it as soon as she got home. But today, instead of pulling her chair up to her desk and steeling herself to enter the dangerous world of homework, she collapsed on her bed and pulled off her necklace so that she could examine it more closely.

Maya had hardly ever taken off the necklace, and she felt strange and vulnerable without its cool surface touching the skin over her heart; it was as if her armor had been pulled off. She held the necklace up to the light that was streaming through the window she had forgotten to close, its precious hue glinting in the afternoon sun.

She pressed her finger to the dove on the front of the necklace, feeling its thin outline, veins that crawled along this golden heart. And then she turned the necklace over, exposing the side that usually rested against her soft, pale skin. She had examined that side of the necklace many times before, often around this time of year. Because, as Scarlett had so truthfully pointed out, around June 10 was the time that Maya became most hungry for a role in the world, for a reason to exist. And yet, this time, she poured even more conviction into her scrutiny.

Etched on the back of the necklace were words

written in a fancy, fragile script. They were in English, one of the many languages taught in school, along with Cloudian, the language of the Land. Staring at the words, Maya willed them to make sense. They were an address, as she had told Scarlett: 15 Harding St., Shellside, UK. Still, she didn't quite understand their purpose. What did 15 Harding Street hold in store?

Beneath the address, miniscule lines drew out the shape of a seashell. Maya had never seen a seashell, of course, because there were none in the Land of the Clouds, but she recognized the intricate design from her classes about Earth. She supposed the seashell came from the name of the town: Shellside.

Even knowing this, Maya was still swirling through the depths of her thoughts, trying, trying, until her head ached, to figure out the connections between everything. She was the person in the prophecy—she was sure of it. All her life, everything had been pointing toward this. How had she not seen it? How had it taken Sir Galiston and Scarlett to bring the pieces together? It was as if she'd been playing one huge game of chess her whole life, making moves that instinctively felt right, and now she could see that they were all part of one master plan. Only, she didn't entirely know what the master plan was.

Maya lay on her bed, thinking, hands covering her face, trying to block the sunlight from distracting her, until she could ignore it no more. The light was now shining severely, painfully, from a west-facing window, like scalding water in her face. It would be time for supper in just about an hour and a half, she thought, and she was sure Auntie would not like her to be late for it again. The very thought of their argument the previous night made the anger in Maya's stomach seethe, nearly overpowering her yearning for a place in the world.

Maya rose from her bed and sat at her desk, looking at her homework as if expecting it to do itself. No, only people with telekinesis could do that. This in turn reminded Maya that she had not discovered her power yet, causing her stomach to flip again. Maya tried to do her homework, she really tried, but she couldn't focus on the altitudes of various important cities on Earth, nor on weather patterns, nor on fractions, and least of all on the questions about the OCT from Sir Galiston.

Eventually, having done none of her homework, and feeling that her stomach had knit itself into an extremely tight knot, Maya heard Auntie call her down to supper.

Maya went willingly that night, and they sat on the porch, enjoying their stew and watching the sun dip down toward the horizon. It dyed the clouds pink and orange, yellow and red as it neared them, shimmering spectacularly as it began to disappear, leaving behind a soft purple wake. Maya could actually hear some neighbors clapping from their porch in the still, rich air.

The conversation at supper was boring, but at least no fights broke out. In fact, Maya rather thought that it seemed like last evening had never happened, which she was grateful for. She tried to shove the thought of the prophecy out of her mind, forcing it out of a door in her head, but it kept popping back in through open windows. She had no intention of bringing it up, no intention of letting Auntie know about the thoughts percolating behind her magical eyes, but she had no hope of stopping the question she eventually asked.

It was innocuous enough, and yet Maya had not meant to ask it. It had simply slipped out in the few minutes before they cleared their plates. "Why were my parents on Earth?"

Frankly, it was a question that Maya had wondered about forever, and she thought of it whenever she woke up in a sweat at night, the vision of disappearing from Earth still in her mind. In that way, she figured that asking it wouldn't necessarily betray her ulterior motive.

Auntie squinted a little and tilted her head, looking peaceful and solemn. The creases and wrinkles on her 200-year-old face seemed to vanish as she pondered Maya's question.

"I suppose it was only a matter of time before you asked that." She sighed. "Your parents," she began carefully, trying to find her footing in what seemed to be mine-filled territory, "were the children of People of the Land. Their families lived on Cloud 14"—for each settlement of the Land was labeled with a number—"which," Auntie continued, "dissolved before you were born." Dissolving—when all of the inhabitants of a certain Cloud decided to pass on, to ascend to the heavens—happened occasionally.

"However," Auntie told Maya, who was beginning to look interested, "your parents were not a part of the People. Their teen years came and went, and they did not show signs of developing magical ability; nor did they display the aptitude for time travel."

Maya was aghast, her breath stolen from her by shock. Her parents had not even been able to do the things she, at eleven, could do. They had never understood how the mere thought of time travel could feel like a connection to your soul, centering you in the midst of a storm. She felt tears bristle, and before she knew it, the speckles of gold and silver in her eyes were rippling, threatening to be drowned by a sob.

Auntie placed a comforting hand on Maya's arm. "I know this must be hard for you to hear. Would you like me to stop?"

Maya shook her head vehemently. "Keep going," she whispered.

"Your parents met and fell in love. They realized they had no life up in the Land. They went to Earth, and they never came back. Then, we heard their cry on that day so many years ago, and we saw you, just a baby. We rescued you, and I offered to care for you. You would have been raised by biological family, but as I already said, the Cloud they lived on dissolved . . ." Her voice drifted off.

"What happened to them?" Maya sniffled and rubbed her nose on her sleeve.

Auntie shook her head. "We don't know. They may be alive . . . we don't know."

Maya nodded her understanding and then asked to be excused. Auntie complied, and Maya fled to her room.

She dropped down on her bed. Her mind was so confused that she couldn't discern whether her thoughts were coming at a hundred miles per hour or hardly moving at all. She had fantasized about her parents for years, but they had always been powerful people, their peculiar existence on Earth something she glossed over with tales of how brave and special they had been.

But they had not been special. They had been more ordinary than everyone she knew. They had been outcasts. Maya felt tainted, as if someone had covered her face in swathes of ugly paint. It hadn't been easy—it wasn't easy— to grow up knowing that she was different, that she didn't have parents to run home to at the end of the day, but she had made the best out of it. She was smart, always one of the best in school, so people didn't really question her past. But if they knew what she had just found out, how would they treat her? How could Maya live with herself knowing these horrible truths?

Crying silently into her pillow, the world darkening to a smooth black all around her, Maya slowly fell into a tortured sleep.

She dreamed again that night. First came the dream of her parents, causing her to sweat and turn and cry out in her sleep. The night air surged in through the window she had yet again forgotten to close, cocooning her in a horrible, icy case. She did not wake up.

Then came a different dream, one she had never experienced before.

She was walking through a meadow full of swaying grasses and delicate flowers. She danced, laughing as the grasses tickled her bare feet and ankles. The sun was smiling down, and warmth seeped into the air. A slight breeze caused her hair to wave and her dress to billow. She grinned, content. She knew she could have easily stood here, inhaling the perfumed aroma of the flowers, all day long and into the night as well.

And then something caught her eye. Something on the edge of the meadow. She had to squint to see it and ran lightly over to take a better look. A forest was growing on the edge of the meadow, and as she watched, new saplings sprang up and sprouted and grew leaves within a second.

Curiosity biting at her heels, she peered around the trunk of a tall tree and then entered the forest. Her eyes widened in shock. She saw a clearing, but not a happy one, with soft green grass and birds chirping—no.

The sun barely reached this space, and it was lit with a dim, grey light. The wind howled fiercely, tearing at her hair. There was something in the center of the clearing, she realized. Thick grey tendrils of mist lashed at whatever was in the center, climbing over each other like deadly vines creeping up a tree. Her breath grew shallow. She heard a shout from inside the cage of mist. Someone was in danger. She had to help them.

But as she began to step forward, tendrils whipped toward her and began encircling her too. They wove around her, darting in and out, stinging her skin. She could feel pressure building. Her ears were close to popping. She tried to step forward one more time, but the tendrils held her back.

They were getting closer. Her head was about to burst. She could hardly breathe. Soon, the tendrils would snake into her throat, her lungs. Her eyes fluttered on the brink of consciousness.

She awoke with a huge intake of breath. Her hands were shaking, and she couldn't stop them. She was freezing cold, but this shivering was from something else entirely. Jumping out of bed to close the window, she felt that her whole body had been jump-started. Her mind was racing. No, not racing—it was snowballing. It was falling down a hill and she had no way to stop it. She paced her room, jittery, unable to stand still. That dream. The memory of it pierced her mind. She had felt so helpless, her attempt to assist resulting in her own capture.

Maya needed to help that person. She needed to. Something was stopping her, but she needed to do it all the same. And then everything clicked into place. Maya stopped pacing, stood still. She was astonished by how quiet the world was outside of her bustling head and hardly dared to move for fear of upsetting the precarious balance she had found. Her powerless parents, taken from her . . . the prophecy . . . the dream . . .

Exactly *when* she realized what she was going to do, Maya had no clue. It just appeared in her head, a fully formed idea. She grabbed her necklace. 15 *Harding St.* That was where she would go. It must have some relation to her parents. She needed to know what had happened to them. *It was a part of the prophecy,* she thought. *It had to be.*

Quickly, hardly thinking, Maya grabbed a bag from her closet and began to pack for her journey to Earth.

No one saw her when she slipped out of the house at 1 a.m. on June 10. No one noticed the small figure prowling the silent, sleepy streets. She was protected by the darkness of the night, by the new moon. Even if someone had happened to peer out their window into the pitch-black night, they wouldn't have thought to look for her.

She wasn't sure how to get to Earth, much less to 15 Harding St. Still, there was only one way she could think of to start her journey and so, taking a deep breath, color flushing her taut cheeks, she perched at the edge of the Land of the Clouds, overlooking the Earth far below, and jumped.

CHAPTER 5

The Beginning

Maya fell through the night, frigid air whirling around her. She could see nothing but could feel the darkness pressing in on her, whispering in her ear. She could see tiny pinpricks of light down beneath, coming from various human towns and cities, she supposed.

As she descended, she felt something change. It was strange, like a combination of being freed from a cage and being released into a storm. It felt like she had burst through a bubble that she had never realized existed. Or like chains, which she had been unaware of, had snapped.

She would have liked to have discovered the meaning of this transition but, considering that she was in the midst of an uncontrolled free fall, now was not the time.

She continued plummeting through the sky, her traveling cloak billowing out above her like a very ineffective parachute. It was the thought of a parachute that raised a fear in her mind. How was she going to stop? How would she make sure that she wasn't going to hit the Earth and flatten herself? Hitting a surface from this high up was sure to be deadly.

The lights below were growing larger and larger, and the dark night around her seemed dense and claustrophobic. She squirmed, flailing, trying to slow her fall. She was forcibly reminded of her dream, of flying *up* into the Land, but quickly pushed the thought out of her mind. The ground was growing closer and closer, and the wind tore at her face, clawing at her eyes, which she struggled to keep open.

She was breathing fast and uncontrollably now. She felt faint, fainter than ever in her life. She wanted to close her eyes and let the darkness sweep her up, take her anywhere but where she was going. In a last-ditch attempt, she snatched the end of her cloak and tried to hold it above her like a parachute. She didn't expect it to work, and she could barely hold on to it, for the wind kept trying to force it out of her grip, but eventually the ground seemed to be approaching in a slower fashion.

Her hands felt as though they had been stabbed with a thousand needles. She was not at all sure that she would be able to move them once she reached the ground.

The Earth, like a ball being thrown at her face, was closer then, right in front of her. Maya could see that she was going to land in a dark patch between a smattering of lights. A forest, probably.

Maya was like an angel falling from heaven as she crashed into the treetops. She grunted and closed her eyes as branches snapped, flicking into her face and digging themselves into her arms and legs, angry to be disturbed. With a great effort that turned her face white, she released her clamp on her cloak-parachute and commanded her hands to instead grab a branch, so she wouldn't fall all the way to the forest floor.

It felt as though her arms were being ripped out of her shoulders, but she held on and was soon dangling from a thick branch, her hands sweaty, scratched, and bleeding from the rough bark, her legs swinging wildly in the air beneath her.

She breathed deeply in and out, willing herself not to let go, not to look down, not to succumb to the stars popping in her vision. Exerting energy she didn't know she had, she swung around to perch on the top of the branch. All people of the Land were far more agile than those on

Earth, and she had the perfect small build for scrambling across the branches of the tree. Wobbling slightly, her vision still blocked by bursting white dots, she clambered to the tree trunk, wrapping her arms around it, sighing in relief to have something solid to steady herself with.

But she was not done yet. There still remained the task of climbing down the tree. This was comparatively easy, however, for she had climbed up and down many trees in the Land. In another minute, she had descended the tree, and her feet touched the ground. The ground. Ground— Earth ground. The ordeal of stopping her fall had caused her to forget where she was falling to. This was not ground in the Land. This was ground on Earth. She was on Earth.

Maya collapsed onto the thin layer of pine needles on the ground. The air was fresh, aromatic with the scent of leaves and nature. It was unlike anything Maya had ever sensed before. She wanted to breathe it in, to never stop smelling Earth, the place she was from. She never wanted to let it go. And yet, there was something else in the air, something that caused Maya to recoil and flare her nostrils. It was oily and grimy. The type of thing you wanted to scrub off your hands until they were red and raw. Maya thought for a moment. Pollution. The stench of pollution hardly ever reached into the Land. *It's disgusting*, she thought.

Maya tried to ignore the pollution for the moment. She lay on the ground and stared up at the sky. Through the thick bramble of branches and leaves, she could barely see the night, but she caught glimpses of clouds far above. Was that Cloud 7, her home?

It seemed so far away now. Maya raised her hand and waved slightly, though she knew no one could see her. *Goodbye for now*, she thought, tears making her eyes smart.

CHAPTER 6

Aftermath

Auntie Flora awoke on June 10 just before the sun reared its head to meet the day. She strode down the hallway, quickly but silently. Maya's door was closed, but Auntie knew she'd be up soon.

She headed to the kitchen, humming under her breath as she put two pieces of toast in the toaster. Then she gathered up her cloak and walked out the front door, closing it softly behind her as she went to pick up the newspaper.

Auntie liked her paper first thing in the morning. Most people waited till their commute to get it, saying it was too cold to go earlier. That may have been true. In fact, it probably was true. Auntie's breath appeared as a puff of condensation in front of her as she walked down the street. But she enjoyed this, found the cold early morning walks to be sleepy and pristine, undisturbed by the din of daily life. Everything was quiet at this time of day. The myriad stars above her were fading slightly, and the sky was a deep indigo now.

Upon reaching the corner store, Auntie found it empty. She called good morning to the owner, who was busy with something in the storeroom, before picking up her paper, tossing a coin in the tip jar, and disappearing back into the predawn world.

Once back at the house, Auntie pulled off her cloak. Her cheeks were flushed from the biting cold outside, but she didn't mind. She set the paper down on the kitchen table, pulled the toast out of the toaster, and with the sun beginning to rise over the horizon, pored over the paper as she waited for Maya to come downstairs.

The newspaper reported that Cloud 7 had moved over northern France during the night and likely would be in that area for a few days. The paper also said that Cloud 28 was expected to be nearby sometime this week, and so if anyone had family or friends they had been thinking of visiting, the time to do so was soon.

Auntie thought. She didn't have any friends or family on Cloud 28, but she recalled that Maya had a friend who had moved there a few years ago. Speaking of Maya, where was she? She was usually up by now. Auntie bit her lip, pondering. Was there any reason that Maya wouldn't get up on time today? It wasn't a holiday, it wasn't the weekend . . .

Oh! June 10! Auntie shook her head, disappointed with herself. How could she have forgotten?

She pulled a chocolate bar out of the pantry and set in next to Maya's plate. Then she took a piece of paper from a drawer and wrote, "Happy eleventh anniversary of living in the Land! We all love you very much!"

But still—where was Maya? She had never missed school on the anniversary before, or missed school for any reason at all.

A bad feeling tickling the back of her head, Auntie traipsed up the stairs and down the hall, coming to a stop in front of Maya's room. She knocked tentatively on the door. No one answered.

Auntie turned the door handle carefully, opening the door a little bit. "Maya?" she called softly. No answer.

Her heart beating loudly in her chest, Auntie threw the door open. Maya's room was empty. Her bed was unmade, looking as though she'd left it in a hurry. Otherwise, though, the room wasn't disturbed. But Auntie immediately noticed Maya's travelling cloak, as well as her backpack, were missing.

Auntie's pulse was now hammering out a code, a message for Maya to come back. *Where had she gone? Why had she gone?* There were no signs of a struggle, and as Auntie stepped around Maya's room, running her hand along the dresser, the desk, she had to admit that she would have known if Maya had been taken by force. Besides, the windows, which locked solely from the inside, were all latched shut.

Auntie ran her hand frantically through her hair. She had to do something. She had to tell someone. Scarlett Clayden. She would go to the Claydens' house. Perhaps Maya was there.

Auntie rushed downstairs and out of the house, leaving the toast on the plates, even forgetting to grab her cloak. There had been a period of weird shock when she had seen that Maya was gone, Auntie thought, ignoring passersby's shouts of "Good morning" as she ran down the street. That moment had passed, and into the absence of feeling that was like an empty pool, worry had flooded.

Auntie arrived in front of the Claydens' a few minutes later and knocked fiercely on the door.

Scarlett came to the door a second later. She looked surprised when she opened it. "Oh, hi! Good morning, Flora!"

"Who is it?" a voice called from inside.

"Flora!" Scarlett shouted back. She turned back to face Auntie. "How are you?" Then she saw Auntie's face, how it was taut with nervousness and worry. "Come in, come in. What's the matter? Is everything okay?"

They stepped into the Claydens' house. Scarlett's mother appeared in the entryway. "Hi, Flora. Is everything okay?"

"Is Maya here?" asked Auntie, looking from mother to

daughter.

"No," Scarlett's mother said slowly. "Why?"

"Oh no," Scarlett exclaimed. She threw her hand over her mouth. "She isn't gone, is she?"

Auntie swallowed. She nodded. "I don't know where," she whispered.

Scarlett looked horror-struck. Her eyes were wide and glassy with tears. Her mother wrapped her arms around her. "It's okay, it's okay," she murmured. Then she turned back to Auntie. "What happened?"

"I don't know." Auntie's voice was trembling. "She didn't show up for breakfast, so I went up to her room. She wasn't there." Her voice crawled into nothingness with the last sentence.

"Oh dear." Scarlett's mother's face was fraught with worry. "Do you think—"

Auntie shook her head heavily. "I don't think she was kidnapped or anything like that. I would've heard. And—" Auntie had to take a deep breath, and Scarlett's mother detached one of her arms from hugging Scarlett to pat Auntie's arm. "A cloak and bag were missing," Auntie finished. "I think—I think she left."

Scarlett's mother's eyes were pouring genuine sympathy. "I don't even know what to say. You have no idea why she would've . . .?" Her voice trailed off.

Scarlett was now sobbing. She mumbled incoherently.

"What, honey?" her mother asked calmly, stroking her hair.

"It's my fault," Scarlett spat out, crying even harder. "It's all my fau—"

"Oh, honey. It's no one's fault, and most certainly not yours," her mother said soothingly.

"Your mom's right," Auntie told her. "Whatever you think, it isn't anyone's fault. What matters now is that we find her."

"But, I—" Scarlett started. Her mom shushed her.

"You'd better go to the police," she told Flora.

"I'll go now. I just hoped... I figured I would check here first."

"Of course, of course. Now, go."

Auntie nodded shakily. "Thank you."

"You're welcome."

Auntie was nearly out the door when Scarlett's mother called after her, "Maya will be found. She'll be okay."

"I know," Auntie replied, trembling. "I know." She turned and, closing the door behind her, started sprinting down the street.

Auntie threw herself through the precinct door, and stood, breathing heavily, at the desk.

"Good morning, ma'am," the officer at the desk said. Her eyes crinkled in a sort of smile.

"Good morning." Auntie tripped over her words. "I'm Flora. Flora Wood.

"What can I do for you, Ms. Wood?"

"Well," Auntie began, attempting to collect herself, "my niece—rather, my ward, Maya Wood—isn't at home. I mean to say that I'm afraid she's run away." Auntie felt tears in her eyes and quickly wiped them away.

The officer, who had been writing notes on a paper, looked up at Auntie. "Sorry. Could you clarify your relationship to Maya?"

Auntie nodded vigorously. "Yes. You see, she is the girl who was brought from Earth. Eleven years ago, I took her in."

"I see. Is there any reason Maya would run away?"

"Not that I'm aware of. She does well in school, and the kids are nice to her. She and I get along, for the most part.

We had a small fight a few days ago, but we've both forgiven each other."

"I see. I'll put people on her case. If you could write down your address, we'll come and check the scene out."

"Thank you, thank you."

"Of course. It's scary," she added, "not knowing where your child is."

Auntie laughed shakily. "Very."

"We'll find her. Just you wait. We'll find her."

CHAPTER 7

Time Travel

Maya spent the rest of the night curled up on the forest floor. As eager as she was to see Earth, she was exhausted. In the morning, she woke to sunlight streaming in through the branches above.

It took her moment to orient herself. But once she had remembered the events of the previous night, she relaxed and began to take in the scenery. Her eyes shone with delight as she peered around the small clearing she was in. The trees were magnificent and tall, spreading their long arms to create a leafy canopy. Although there were trees in the Land of the Clouds, Maya had never seen this many in one place.

She sighed as she stood up, feeling the solid earth beneath her feet. It was so firm, so reliable. Unlike the clouds, it was always in one place, never drifting away. Maya pulled her provisions out of the backpack she had brought. She was carrying enough food for a few days, as well as a canteen of water and a blanket.

She had thought she was prepared, but she had no idea what to expect when she left the forest, for she knew she would have to leave eventually. She wanted to see the rest of the Earth. And, of course, she wanted to find 15 Harding Street.

This thought brought Maya's hand unconsciously to her chest, where the necklace lay between her tunic and skin. She felt her cheeks flush with excitement. She was here—she was actually on Earth, the place where she was from. She was the one in the prophecy, and she was going to find out what had happened to her parents.

A nagging, pessimistic voice in her head wormed its way forward. *How are you going to do that, little girl?* it hissed.

Maya, who had been repacking her bag, paused. How was she going to do that?

Maya chewed that over as she began wandering through the forest. She felt like she knew the answer, like it was hiding right in front of her, behind one of the bushes plump with berries.

At the edge of the forest, the dark, dense green gave way to a sunny, warm field, and Maya wondered where she was, *when* she was. And then it struck her, a bolt of lightning out of the sky.

Time, she thought. *Time travel. I can time travel now!*

She thought back to the peculiar sensation she had felt while falling through the air the previous night, the feeling that she had been freed. Had that been the feeling of passing into Earth, where she would finally be able to time travel?

All thought of exiting the forest wiped from her mind, Maya felt her body buzz with anticipation as she prepared. She was about to try time travel, actual time travel, for the first time. She had partially entered into this state of mind before, back in the Land, but it had been like stepping into cold water and having the waves force you back out onto the beach. She hoped that this time she would be able to submerge herself.

A flicker of doubt crossed Maya's mind, a dark cloud blotting out the sun. Her breath came fast, wavering. *You can't do this*, the pessimistic voice whispered, digging a hole of uncertainty in Maya's mind. *You've never done this before. Just flee the forest, little girl. Call to the sky for help. Go back to the Land.*

No, Maya thought, summoning her energy, forcing

that voice out. *No, I can do this.* And with that, she plunged.

Concentrating as if her life depended on it, Maya let herself sink, and soon she could feel icy waves lapping at her feet. She was standing on a grey beach, surrounded by the roar of the wind of time. The chirps of birds and the rustle of leaves in the forest began to fade away.

Focusing all of her energy, Maya took a step forward into the cold water. It stung her ankles, and she could feel it digging into her skin. And yet she felt no barrier. The waves were not pushing her away.

Maya took another step. She was knee-deep in the waves, no longer able to hear anything but the wind. She was shivering and yet sweating from the effort it took.

Maya began to place her foot forward again, but something stopped her, something she sensed at the edge of her vision. Cautiously, the wind ripping at her tunic, Maya peered down into the water. She could barely see through it, but she knew. About a foot from where she stood, cold, nervous, the sandbar she was on dropped off. There would be no more steps. She would have to dive. And so, barely able to breathe for the fear and tension nestled in her chest, Maya closed her eyes and dived.

The cold hit her, smacked her, throttled her, but she didn't stop. She pushed through the water, going deeper, deeper. After what felt like an hour, Maya gave up and opened her eyes. She could not bear being unable to see her surroundings, cocooned in the dark of her eyelids.

What she saw in front of her caused her to gasp. She breathed in, forgetting she was underwater, but found that she could inhale and exhale as normally as if she were on land. This distracted her attention for a mere moment before she refocused on the sight before her.

Where there should have been darkness, the murky depths of the ocean, there was instead light. Scenes were being played out on water rippling by. Maya saw a fire rage to her right, and men with weapons charging at her from her left. The pictures, the snapshots, continued down, down, down, and Maya knew that she was looking at the Tunnel of Time.

She smiled. She almost laughed. Her eyes were alight, reflecting the scenes all around her, memories of time, of the past, going back and back. She, Maya, an eleven-year-old, was in the Tunnel of Time. She could go anywhere in history she wanted. Of course, she could only view the history of the area near the forest she had been in when she left—something she had learned in class in the Land—but the opportunities still seemed endless.

Maya swam deeper, her eyes wide open with excitement as she traveled through time. She spun around in the water, which was still cold, though not as bothersome, and looked up at the front of the tunnel.

Far above, a shaft of light hit the surface of the ocean. From her classes, Maya knew that she could swim all the way to the surface, and when she emerged, she would be back in the forest in whatever time period she'd originally landed in. However, Maya had no intention of going back to that time; she wanted to explore.

It seemed the tunnel would never end. She went deeper and deeper, but the excitement of the tunnel was beginning to fade away. She wanted to enter one of the memories, to be transported to that time. She had not thought of the necklace, of 15 Harding Street, since before she had gone to the grey beach and was not thinking of it now. She merely wanted a bit of adventure, something that would prove she was old enough to time travel successfully, that everyone in the Land had been wrong.

This desire to show everyone she was right sparked the embers in her stomach. Her eyes glinting fiercely, she launched herself through the nearest scene—two knights on horses running at each other, lances in their hands.

As soon as her head hit the scene, splitting the picture in half, a rush of water hit her from behind. It propelled her, sending her zooming through the icy-cold ocean.

She twisted and turned, unable to tell where she was going, panic rising in her throat. Then all of a sudden she was back on the grey beach, about ten feet from the water. She looked down at herself. She was inexplicably dry, her bag still slung over her shoulders, and cold only because of the wind around her.

Nervously, she turned in a circle. How was she supposed to leave the beach? They have never covered this in school. As she thought it, a burst of wind hit her in the face. She heard shouts in the distance, as if through a long tunnel.

Unsure of what she was doing, swallowing hesitantly while the nagging voice in her head pushed its way to the front once again, she furrowed her brow, concentrating on leaving the beach and appearing in the scene with two knights.

Slowly but surely, the beach began to fade. The shouts grew louder and the wind quieter.

She closed her eyes to concentrate. *Out, out, out . . .*

It was as if a bubble had popped. She loosened her grip on her focus and immediately fell over. Opening her eyes, scared of what she would find, her heart pounding in her chest, she looked around. She was still at the edge of the forest, but the scene in the field was different; it was now full of people and noise. She glimpsed two knights on horses charging at each other, wisps of wind curling around them, mild in the summer air. She grinned, feeling as light and airy as the day. Her eyes were bright with joy.

She lay down on the forest floor, tired but happy. She

had done it. She had done what everyone said she couldn't. She had time traveled.

CHAPTER 8

The Second Beginning

Auntie sat in a blue plastic chair in the waiting area of the police precinct. Running her fingers through her long silver hair, she couldn't keep focused. She couldn't focus on the tree outside the window, nor the polished, tiled floor of the precinct, nor any other thing that the officer at the desk had suggested focusing on to keep her mind off of Maya's disappearance.

The officer had said that one of her colleagues would go over to the house with Auntie in an attempt to find clues to what had happened. Auntie glanced frantically at her watch, her knee bouncing up and down. It was 8:10. That had been ten minutes ago.

Auntie sighed frustratedly. She was worried—beyond worried. It was as though the world had come crashing down when Maya left. And where was she? Auntie hoped with all her heart that her niece was safe, that she would come home soon. A tear dripped down Auntie's face, solitary, gleaming in the morning light. She sniffled slightly.

The officer at the desk looked kindly over at her. "Do you need a tissue?" she asked softly.

Auntie opened her mouth to respond, but before she could say anything, a door behind the officer's desk burst open. Another officer entered the room. The officer at the desk looked up mildly.

"There you are," she said, trying unsuccessfully to hide the tinge of annoyance in her voice. "It's been ten minutes."

The second officer's lip twitched. "Well . . ." he said,

seeming at a loss for words. "I'm here now."

The officer at the desk rolled her eyes slightly in exasperation. "She's over there," she said, pointing to Auntie.

The officer strolled over to Auntie. He seemed about thirty and was as thin as a stick. His badge read "Michaels."

"Hello," Michaels said, holding his hand out to shake Auntie's, who was trying to wipe the tears from her eyes in the most inconspicuous way.

"Hi," Auntie said, shaking his hand. Her voice shook slightly, like the end of a diving board.

"I'm Officer Michaels. I'll be assisting you today."

"Great! Thank you!" Auntie forced out, mustering enthusiasm she didn't feel as she stood up, her back aching slightly. "I'm Flora. Flora Wood."

"A pleasure to meet you, Ms. Wood," Michaels told Auntie, holding the door open for her.

"Yes. You as well."

Outside, the sun was shining brightly, the sky a cotton-candy blue as usual. The wind danced playfully in the air. Altogether, Auntie thought, it was too nice of a day given the ordeal she was going through.

As they strolled down the sidewalk, Michaels said, "Ms. Wood, could you please recall the events leading up to this? It would be awfully helpful for me."

"Of course," Auntie replied, shoving a polite smile onto her face.

Auntie proceeded to retell the events of the morning for what she believed to be the third time, and when she was done, they had already reached the house.

Auntie showed Officer Michaels around the place, assuring him that she and Maya got along and that this was a safe household, while Michaels scrutinized seemingly random things, such as the kitchen counter or the living room sofa. "You never know where you'll find a clue hidden," he informed her.

Upstairs, Auntie pulled open the door to Maya's room and they went in. Michaels wandered around the room, staring at certain spots, seeming to have infinite patience. How could he just stand there and stare at a fleck of paint next to the window? Auntie wondered. How could he seem so relaxed, so calm, when Auntie's heart kept alternating between melting into a puddle on the floor and exploding from her chest?

To Auntie, it seemed that Officer Michaels wasn't discovering anything new about Maya's absence. In fact, Auntie thought that there wasn't anything else to learn. Maya had left. The question Auntie now cared most about, having decided that Maya had not been kidnapped, was: where was she?

Auntie stood in the doorway of Maya's room, watching Officer Michaels, her eyes flitting around distractedly. There was a crack on the ceiling. Michaels had a shock of grey in his dark hair. Auntie sighed, sick of feeling helpless. The idea that she, Maya's guardian, was irrelevant in this matter seemed to make everything worse.

The doorbell rang. Auntie, relieved to have an excuse to be somewhere, and to do something to take her mind off of Maya, went to answer the door. Scarlett was standing on the front stoop, her cheeks flushed, her eyes red.

"Scarlett?" Auntie exclaimed. "What are you doing? You're supposed to be in school!"

Scarlett's eyes were pits of tears. "I-I—"

"All right, all right. Come in," Auntie relented. "But I'm calling your mom."

Scarlett nodded submissively, and the two of them went inside and sat down at the kitchen table.

"Who is it?" Officer Michaels called, his voice echoing

from upstairs.

"Just one of Maya's friends, Officer," Auntie responded tiredly.

"Oh, good." There were footsteps upstairs; Michaels was walking down the hall. "I could ask her—"

"Officer, this girl is very upset. Please save your questions for later," Auntie implored.

"Of course." He sounded defeated, and they heard footsteps retreating a moment later.

"Now, Scarlett," Auntie said, resting her elbows on the kitchen table, "before I call your mother, what's the matter?"

Scarlett was nearly gasping for breath now. "It's my fault," she cried softly.

"It is not." Auntie's brow creased, emphasizing her point.

"But—"

"Listen. Just calm down, Scarlett," Auntie said soothingly. "We're all worried about Maya, and the police are doing everything they can to find her." Tears were prickling at Auntie's eyes.

"They won't," Scarlett whispered, barely making a sound. "I know where she went"—Scarlett put her head in her hands—"and they won't find her."

"What do you mean they won't find her?" Auntie felt her vision sway, and her tone became panicked. "Is she—?"

"She's alive," Scarlett said miserably, "but not safe."

"How do you know?"

"We got in a fight yesterday—" began Scarlett.

"That's not your fault," Auntie told her quietly.

"—about the prophecy."

"About the prophecy?" This conversation was going very differently than Auntie had expected it to. She couldn't deny that her curiosity was piqued—almost, for a moment, overruling her worry.

"Yes, the prophecy." Scarlett sounded tired. She had lifted her head, and Auntie could see her face, puffy and red. "The 'born on the first of two' one."

"Why?" Maya had never brought up the prophecy around Auntie.

Scarlett heaved a great sigh and looked into Auntie's eyes. Scarlett's own irises were solemn and accepting, a forest that knew it was about to be mowed down. "Maya thinks she's the one in the prophecy."

"No . . ."

Scarlett nodded grimly.

Auntie could see the pieces coming together, clicking into place, just as they had the night before for Maya.

"Oh, Maya . . ." Auntie whispered, as if willing her niece to appear on the doorstep like Scarlett had.

Scarlett fidgeted with her fingers. "I'm—I'm sorry for telling you this," she mumbled, looking weary and depressed.

"No, Scarlett, thank you."

Scarlett perked up at these words.

"I had no clue where she was, and I doubt that bozo upstairs was going to be able to help me. But about Maya," Auntie asked tentatively. "Do you mean to say that she's on Earth now?"

Scarlett nodded slowly, as if a heavy weight was around her head. "And," the girl said, "she thinks it all has something to do with her parents. She kept fingering her necklace and talking about the address on the back."

Auntie inhaled, filling her lungs with air, and then exhaled in one great breath. "Well," she said to the mostly empty room, "I'm going after her."

A sense of direction had been instilled in Auntie. Maya was her North, and for a moment, she hadn't known where North was. Now she had found it again.

"You're what?"

"I'm going to Earth to find her. I know I can." Auntie was confident. "I'll leave tonight," she proclaimed, feeling younger than she had in decades.

Scarlett looked aghast. "But I didn't mean for you to—"

"Scarlett. I will find Maya, and we will come home."

Scarlett cast her eyes down. "Fine. But"—she swallowed hesitantly—"do you think she's the one in the prophecy?"

"I don't know. But I do know that Maya will be coming home. Officer Michaels!" Auntie called up the stairs.

The officer appeared at the end of the hallway. "Yes, Ms. Wood?"

"I—I don't think that we require your services anymore."

"I'm sorry?"

"Well"—Auntie thought for a moment, debating whether or not to tell the truth—"Scarlett, Maya's friend, has just informed me that Maya went down to Earth. I intend to go after her and find her."

"To Earth?" Officer Michaels looked shocked. "With all due respect, Ms. Wood, it's the job of the police to track down missing persons."

"She's not missing, though."

"She's on Earth! Earth is huge! And," Michaels added, "I'm not entirely sure if I believe this Scarlett."

Auntie's mind was racing on what to say. "Okay. Fine if you don't believe me! Um, but I'll go to Earth, and you keep looking here!"

Auntie bit her lip in anticipation of what Officer Michaels would say.

Michaels sighed audibly. "I guess that would be okay. The precinct can give you a license to go to Earth, and I'll have to run it all by my superior, but . . ."

In her head, Auntie pumped her fist in the air. Having another person around would just screw up her compass. And Auntie *needed* to find Maya. Behind her newfound determination, there was a pit of fear, and that fear wasn't going to go away unless she found Maya.

Officer Michaels clomped down the stairs—he had surprisingly heavy steps for a man with the physique of a leaf—and headed for the door. "Ms. Wood, could you stop by the precinct this afternoon?"

"Of course."

With that, Officer Michaels took his leave.

"And you, Scarlett," said Auntie, turning to the girl beside her, "you need to go to school."

Scarlett nodded dutifully, her face still puffy. She walked to the door and looked back at Auntie sitting alone at the kitchen table. "Thank you. And *please* don't tell my mother."

"We'll see," Auntie said.

Scarlett nodded again and left, a look of great concern etched upon her young face.

———————————

Auntie glanced at her watch. It was 8:50. She stood up at the kitchen table and looked around. The house felt empty and soulless without Maya. But not for long. At 9 p.m. on June 10, Auntie would take a tunnel down to Earth, landing somewhere in France, in hopes of finding Maya. She had secured her license from the police that afternoon, along with a teleporter that would allow her to move swiftly across Earth.

Auntie walked to the front door, the floorboards creaking slightly. She turned off the lights, and the house was thrown into complete darkness, the only light coming from the stars above. It felt so weird to be leaving the house, going on an adventure, without knowing when she'd be back. To add to that, Auntie and Maya would probably return only about half a day after they left, no matter how long they were gone for.

Outside, the Land was dark and sleepy. Auntie could picture Maya stealing away, launching herself over the edge of the clouds and down to Earth—for that was the only way she could've left. Auntie hoped, hoped with all her heart, that Maya had brought something to slow her fall. If she hadn't . . . The idea was too terrible to think of.

Auntie was partway down the street when something lunged at her from a bush. She nearly screamed, but stopped herself just in time. Scarlett stood in front of her, eyes wild, holding a backpack.

"What are you doing?" Auntie hissed.

"Coming with you." Scarlett's voice was firm, determined. She had clearly been thinking about this for most of the day. "Maya's my friend, and it's my fault she's gone."

"It is not your fault. And I'm taking you home."

"No, please," Scarlett begged. "I want to come!"

"Does your mother know?"

"No, but . . ."

"You're not coming." Auntie began striding down the street. Scarlett jogged to keep up with her.

"I can help. I can use my power to see where Maya is," Scarlett said hopefully.

"How?" Auntie didn't want to be rude, but now did not feel like the time for niceties. "Your power only works with an object."

"And in dreams too, when the object is nearby. Besides, I can see more than just an object now; I can see people who have a connection to the object."

Auntie stopped in her tracks. "Really?" she enquired.

"I didn't know."

"I found out about a month ago. I didn't tell Maya—she got so jealous about those things."

"*Gets*," corrected Auntie, starting to walk again.

"Sorry?"

"*Gets*, not *got*. Maya isn't dead."

"Right, of course. Gets."

They were drawing close to the transport building, where Auntie would take a tunnel to Earth. Auntie considered Scarlett's offer. It might be nice to have a companion, especially one with a convenient power . . .

"You can come," Auntie said abruptly.

"I can . . ."

"You can come with me, Scarlett."

Auntie could see Scarlett grinning in the dark. "Oh, thank you, thank you!" she said excitedly.

"Now, come on."

Auntie used her license to get into the transport building, which was empty, as it was technically after hours, and Scarlett slipped in behind her. By the time anyone realized Scarlett was missing, the duo would already be gone.

CHAPTER 9

The Village with the Knights

Cautiously, Maya inched toward the rim of the forest, yearning for a better view of the tournament on the field. Twigs crunched beneath her feet, and the wind swept her hair over her shoulder as she tiptoed along.

Peering out from behind a mammoth tree trunk, her eyes sparkled in excitement. She could see the people at the tournament more clearly now; they were dressed in rough, cotton clothes.

Her heart pounded. These were real people, actual human beings. She had never met a human before—not that she could remember, at least—and she was eager to see what they were like.

Slowly, she crept out from under the cover of the trees. She ducked low and sprinted across the field, her bag bouncing on her back, to where the people were congregated.

There were murmurs of excitement all around her as she pushed her way through the crowd aimlessly, wanting to see as many humans as possible. Far above her head, a horn sounded, and she heard the thunder of hooves. Her eyes widened in fright at the noise before she realized that the horses were not going to charge into the crowd. Then she continued meandering.

She was endlessly amazed by the people she saw. They were like rocks on a riverbank: mostly the same, but with unique variances. One man had an unusually large nose, and she had to fake a cough to stifle her laughter as he turned to his wife and said something in a remarkably nasally voice. A woman who was watching over five children had beady eyes and large ears like a goblin, and two of her children appeared to be the same person—with identical blond hair, stubby noses, and long legs. Maya goggled at them. Before long, though, one of the children noticed her staring and began to tug on the goblin lady's dress. Maya disappeared back into the crowd.

The air was heavy with sweat, and wafts of smoke kept drifting over. The atmosphere was thick, tangible, real. It felt as solid as the ground beneath Maya's feet, unlike in the Land of the Clouds, where the air was lofty and light like the clouds upon which it perched.

She fought her way to the front of the crowd to see the action up close. Two knights, each in shining silver armor, were sitting on top of the horses. Sitting! On the horses! She had never seen such a thing before, and she laughed out loud. The man beside her frowned at her, and the smile on her face was swallowed up. She coughed nervously, suddenly aware that she did not belong on Earth. It had been fun to wander amongst the people, but that was only when they didn't notice her. The man's eyes felt like fire burning into her flesh, branding her. It seemed like he was expecting her to fly or do something else magical. She cast her eyes down at the dirt beneath her—*real dirt!*—and he looked away. The heat passed.

She watched in fascination as the knights ran at each other, spurring the horses on, but part of her was detached, uncomfortable. She was unable to forget the look the man had given her, though he couldn't have known that she wasn't from Earth, and decided to leave the tournament and explore this area more.

As she pushed her way out of the throngs of people, she began to wonder where she was, when she was. Well, she knew she was in France, but when? It wouldn't do to ask one of these people, for they were certain to become suspicious that she didn't know what year it was.

A village lay beyond the crowd, something that she hadn't noticed in her rush to see humans. She jogged down a wide dirt road, past farms and scattered houses, watching the thatched roofs grow closer.

The village, fields, and forest seemed to be located in a valley, for behind the village there was a peaceful, grassy hill. Her eyes ventured up the slope as she came closer to the village.

At the crest of the hill sat a castle. Her eyes widened and her stomach flipped pleasantly. A castle! She had never seen a castle before! The rough, grey stone outer wall had to be at least thirty feet tall, and there was a tall tower at either front corner of the fortress. The silver and gold in her eyes shone dazzlingly in the summer sunlight. Oh, she would have loved to climb that hill and visit the castle! It would have been incredible! Alas, she knew that she could not, that only people with invitations could visit such magnificent buildings. She sighed sadly, then redirected her energy to the labyrinthine village streets.

After taking several wrong turns, Maya found her way to the village center, where the alternating dirt and cobblestone roads gave way to a grassy plot of land. She ran toward it and collapsed on the prickly grass, still wet with dew.

She gazed up at the brilliant blue sky. It was just like the sky back in the Land. Except for one thing. Clouds flitted across the sky here. Clouds. Other than in her dream, or memory, she had never seen clouds overhead in real life. She tilted her head wonderingly, the sense of elation that she'd feeling ebbing slightly. She couldn't decide whether she liked the clouds or not. They seemed like giant pieces of candy floss, all puffy and round. And yet . . .

There was something off about them. Something that made them feel dark and moody. Maybe it was that she knew she was only seeing their underside, that she knew there was a whole other world above them. It was the strangest feeling, to be watching her world from beneath, to be in a whole other world.

Earth was fabulous. She felt that fire burning in her stomach. She had proved herself, she thought. She had gone off and carved her own path. That was even more impressive than the knights jousting or the royal castle on the hill.

She was falling into a bit of a daze, her eyes unfocused, her body firmly against the ground in this magical, sun-warmed spot. Earth *was* magical, even more magical than the Land, she said to herself, her thoughts beginning to slur. Somewhere in the very back of her mind, she knew that she couldn't stay on this vacation forever, that she had to complete the prophecy, find 15 Harding St.

But, she thought, *that could be an adventure for another day*. Her eyes closed softly and she was lost in the world of sleep.

Before she knew it, she was awake, the sun having hardly moved in the sky. A rough hand was shaking her shoulder. She sat straight up, her hand around her bag. "What?" The word sounded twisted, as her mouth tried to catch up with her brain.

The person shaking her was a large, heavyset man in a butcher's apron. A scowl was etched into his face. "What did you say?"

Her brain was thinking overtime. She had spoken in Cloudian by accident. What language was he speaking? French, she decided. Old French.

"I'm sorry," she began, trying to adjust her accent to match the butcher's.

"You can't sleep here. Get up, or I'll go to the sheriff." The man lifted a club with his other hand and smacked it menacingly against his palm.

"I-I'm very sorry, sir," she said hastily, standing up. "I'll leave."

"No! Wait." The man inspected Maya's face, his own purple one leaning in close. "Where are you from?" The question could have sounded harmless, but instead it sounded murderous.

"Um, here," she lied, hoping her voice wasn't shaking. She clutched her bag tighter, and her heart sprinted fast in her chest.

"No, you're not! Your accent . . ." The butcher looked thoughtful, or, as thoughtful as he could. "I'm getting the sheriff. Stay here!" he bellowed, then turned on his heel.

Maya was dizzy from hunger and about to get in serious trouble. If the man got the sheriff, they would undoubtedly see through her lies. Then what? Would she be tortured? Forced to give up the location of the Land of the Clouds? Her thoughts snowballed.

Soon, the butcher reappeared with someone dressed in official-looking clothing, who must've been the sheriff. Maya was desperate. How could she get out? How could she get out? Then the idea flew to her. Time travel.

She lowered herself into that weird state once more, and soon she was on the grey beach. The voices of the men were echoing distantly.

"She's fading, look!"

"She's disappearing!"

"Witch!"

"Get the witch!"

"What's happening?"

"Kill her!"

Maya's heart stopped for a moment as she heard

the last words, and she shuddered. Then she pressed on, forcing herself to run into the icy water. This time it was much easier to wade through the waves, and she didn't hesitate to jump in at the end of the sandbar.

Maya swam faster than she ever had before, eyes open, breathing. She didn't know if she could be caught in real life, and she didn't want to find out. Faster, faster she pushed herself, the water turning her toes numb, her eyes streaming. *Please*, she thought. *Let me see the Tunnel of Time.* But it did not appear. She kept swimming, kept praying: *Please, please, please.*

She closed her eyes to blink the tears out of them, and when she opened them, she saw the tunnel going down, down, down. This time, however, she didn't explore, didn't watch the scenes in fascination. She simply dove through the first scene she saw, not caring what was on the other side.

CHAPTER 10

Searching

Scarlett zoomed through darkness, the pressure feeling like taut vines that wrapped around her. She wanted to scream in fright, wanted to betray the erratic beat of her heart, but she did not—could not.

After what felt like an eternity, she was abruptly spit out of the tunnel. There had been no light at the end of the tunnel; the crashing darkness had simply fallen away like curtains dropping to the floor, and then she was sprawled in a field, her head throbbing.

Auntie stood a little ways away, and when she saw Scarlett, she rushed over. "Are you okay? You look like you hit the ground pretty hard."

"Yeah, I'm fine." The words vibrated in Scarlett's head.

Scarlett sat up, one hand to her forehead, as if afraid her skull might split open without something to stop it. She looked around. It was night, as it had been in the Land. But this darkness was nothing like it had been in the tunnel; here it was light and airy, a soft wind blowing through it, waving the grasses on the ground in a hypnotic pattern. Earth.

She turned to Auntie, her head pounding. She winced. "Where are we?"

"Somewhere in France, I suppose. Now, let's get going immediately. There's no time to waste." Auntie turned around, hiking her backpack up on her shoulders, and made to walk away.

Scarlett groaned behind her.

Auntie turned to face her. "What is it?"

"My head." Scarlett could barely speak because of the pain, which had increased tenfold since a moment ago. "I must've hit it . . ." Scarlett's voice trailed off as her eyes glazed over. She slumped and was unconscious, her hair glinting in the moonlight.

Auntie gasped slightly and then kneeled down beside Scarlett and felt her forehead. It wasn't particularly hot. That was good; it meant Scarlett had most likely just banged her head. People of the Land were not hurt nearly as easily as humans, and when Scarlett woke up, she was undoubtedly going to feel fine. Nevertheless, Auntie rummaged in her bag, digging past a sheathed dagger to find an herbal salve that would help. She spread the gooey green paste over Scarlett's forehead and then sat down, tapping her finger mindlessly against the ground, anxious for Scarlett to wake so they could get going.

Auntie stared up at the night sky, eager for something to take her mind off of Maya's absence. When she was on the go, actually progressing in finding her niece, the waves of worry couldn't sweep her off her feet. But right now . . .

The stars above twinkled faintly; they looked much hazier than they did in the Land. Auntie scowled. Pollution. She was trying to find some of the constellations when there was a gasp beside her.

Auntie pulled out her dagger and whirled around to see Scarlett sitting up, panting. Her eyes were wild in the darkness.

"Scarlett!" Auntie cried. "Are you okay?"

"Yes, yes, fine," Scarlett told her hurriedly. "I had a dream."

"A dream?" Auntie mentally raised an eyebrow but kept a straight face.

"Yes, that comes from my power . . ." Scarlett said, sounding like Auntie ought to have remembered this.

"Of course. Right." Auntie was more interested now. She wiped the salve off of Scarlett's forehead. "What was the dream?"

"I don't know how but . . . I saw Maya."

"Maya?! Is she okay?" Auntie's voice was fraught with worry.

Scarlett nodded. "She was in this place . . . I don't know . . . an old village, maybe? It looked like it was from Earth's Middle Ages. Only . . . I don't know how I saw her. Did you bring something that belongs to her?"

Auntie gave a small gasp and reached into her backpack, retrieving the sheathed dagger. Every person in the Land of the Clouds was given their own dagger at birth, though most parents rightly locked their children's up until they were eighteen. "This is Maya's. I brought it for when we find her. Do you think this could have prompted your dream?"

Scarlett nodded.

"Maya must've time traveled," Auntie said quietly. She simultaneously found this impossible and entirely plausible. On the one hand, Maya was constantly rebelling. But didn't she know that there was a reason eleven-year-olds weren't allowed to time travel?

"What are we going to do?" Scarlett's voice, nervous and small, dragged Auntie out of her thoughts.

"Go after her. We came here to find Maya, and that's what we're going to do."

"Right, right. So we're going to time travel?"

Auntie rolled her eyes in her head. "Yes, we'll time travel."

"I've never time traveled before, though." Scarlett's voice shrank as she talked.

"No time like the present," Auntie told her. "Besides, I'm sure you've learned the basics in school."

Scarlett nodded, biting her lip.

"Right. So—what is the scene that we'll be traveling to? Do you know?" Auntie asked. "That way, we won't get stuck in different places in time."

"It's a joust," Scarlett said. "Look for a joust on a summer's day. There's a big crowd, a village nearby, and a castle on a hill, though you might not be able to see the last two." Her voice shook.

"Okay. Remember, you can do this. I know you can. Are you ready?"

Scarlett swallowed and nodded.

"Let's go."

CHAPTER 11

The Slate Building

Scarlett watched as Auntie began to fade away. She held her breath and focused all of her energy on sinking into that strange place. Soon the field around her disappeared and Scarlett was standing on a sidewalk. A tepid rain was pelting her. It stung her skin and seemed to soak into her bones. A slate building stood in front of her, vibrant trees and bushes encircling it. Scarlett stepped forward, toward a revolving glass door.

Now came the hardest part came. Scarlett had never managed to get into the building before, the door always shunting her back around to the exit. Firmly, carefully, Scarlett stepped into the revolving door. The echo of the wind back in the field got quieter as Scarlett poured her energy into moving the door. She could feel beads of sweat dripping down her face, a combination of effort and humid air. Finally, her legs aching, Scarlett was spit out into the building's lobby. Her hands were clammy, her head dizzy. This was it. She was there. In the building.

Scarlett had often imagined how it would feel to be there, on the other side, how it would be cool and airy, not stuffy as it was outside. She was wrong. The air inside the building was, if at all possible, worse than it had been outside. It seemed stagnant, poisoned, and hot. It clung to Scarlett's braids, to her tunic, to every bit of her skin; she could barely breathe. And still she kept walking. It had become easier to move now. She ran across the deserted lobby, empty of both furniture and people. Her footsteps, which should have rung clearly on the marble floor, were muffled.

At the end of the lobby there was a door. A door! She bolted for it, desperate for a respite from the boiling lobby. She swung the door open. It was thick and heavy, just like everything in the room. She peered beyond it. There was a dark spiral staircase leading down, down, down. She stepped onto the landing and looked around. The door slammed shut behind her, leaving her in the dark. She stepped down a single stair, somehow unafraid of the darkness. The air was cooler already, light and breathable, and she could hear the echo of her step. Tentatively, she took another step. And another, and another.

The walls, which had been a smooth black stone, suddenly lit up with moving pictures. Scenes played out in front of her. She looked up, looked down. The stairs continued above the landing, going up and up until they reached what must have been the roof. A crack of light shone through. Below her, the stairs went on and on, as did the pictures on the walls. And she knew. Her arms and legs buzzed with joy. She had reached the Tunnel of Time.

As much as she would have loved to wander the stairs forever, she had a mission. She descended down past glimpses of cities, summer droughts, battles, and fairs until she reached the scene that had been engraved in her mind since the dream of Maya.

Two knights were jousting. Scarlett stared at the wall. She knew what she had to do, as hesitant as she was. Eyes squeezed closed, teeth gritted, Scarlett ran her head into the wall.

And fell.

And fell.

And fell.

Through pitch-black tunnels she zoomed until suddenly she dropped out of the rainy, humid sky and was standing on the sidewalk in front of the slate building.

She could hear sounds in the distance, echoing from far away. Shouts and laughs. The earthquake of horses' hooves on solid land. With all her might, Scarlett willed herself to rise from the rainy sidewalk, and before she knew it, she was lying on solid ground.

The air was hot and dry. Scarlett sat up on the yellowed grass. Auntie was a few feet away.

Scarlett ran her hand over the ground. Her head was feeling fine; it had been since she'd woken up and . . . she had just time traveled! Actually time traveled! She beamed at Auntie, at the Earth around her. She had forgotten: she was on Earth!

She bounced up, lifting her backpack over her shoulder. Auntie stood as well, though a little creakily. "How was it?" she asked.

"Oh, fabulous!" Scarlett replied. "It was just incredible! It was so powerful, just—" Scarlett shuddered in excitement. "I never thought I would be time traveling at age eleven!"

Auntie smiled.

"Well, let's go find Maya, then!" Auntie exclaimed. "You said you saw her in the village?"

"Yes, in the town square! Come on!"

Scarlett led the way through the mass of people watching the joust, her attention focused on finding her friend. She supposed that, before Maya had gone missing, she would've loved to just wander the Earth with her friend by her side. Now, though . . . there were more important things.

Auntie and Scarlett ran down the road into the village, barely pausing to look at the massive castle on the hill.

In the village, Scarlett led the way; she remembered every shop, every house from her dream. "Say," she said to Auntie, who was walking briskly beside her, "why are we in such a hurry? It's not like we're going to miss Maya, because if we do, we could just go back in time to when she was here, right?"

"Well, no," Auntie explained. "We are not creatures that are supposed to exist in Earth's time. We *don't* exist in Earth's time. It's complicated, but basically, we bring our present self wherever we travel in time or space, and we don't ever stay in the past, even if we visited it. We only exist in a place or time while we are actually in it. Maya was here, but if she has gone"—Auntie took a deep breath and swallowed before continuing—"if she's gone elsewhere, we won't find her here."

Scarlett didn't entirely understand. "Okay . . ."

"I know. It's complicated."

By this point they were close to reaching the town square with its small, cheerful green. Both of their hearts fluttered with hope. Their breathing was shallow. *Please*, Scarlett prayed. *Let me find my friend.*

But then . . .

"Where is she?" Auntie choked on the words.

The green was deserted. There was no hint of an eleven-year-old with green eyes and a determination to break the rules.

"I—I don't know." Scarlett was crestfallen. More than crestfallen. "Maybe she's just down the street. I'll check."

Scarlett sprinted over to the butcher's shop, Auntie following behind her.

The butcher was standing at the counter in his shop, glaring at them as they entered. "What do you want?" he growled.

Scarlett's eyes scanned the small room. The walls were plain and white, and there was a stench of raw meat in the air. "Excuse me, sir," she said timidly, mustering the best Old French she could. "But have you seen a girl about my size recently?"

"Oh, more of you." The butcher's voice dripped with venom, and his scowl became even more pronounced. "You strange people come into this village with your weird accents. And you disappear. Like witches."

Auntie gasped.

"You are like that girl, eh? Wait here, I'm getting the sheriff. *Again*," he added as an afterthought. Then he stalked off, leaving Auntie and Scarlett alone.

"She's gone," croaked Auntie. "We missed her."

Scarlett's eyes filled with tears. "I'm so sorry. If I hadn't hit my head—"

"We wouldn't have known to come here in the first place," Auntie whispered. "We will find her. She has to be somewhere."

"Right." Tears spilled down Scarlett's face. "I just thought that—"

"Me too, me too."

They saw no reason to wait for the sheriff, who was sure to imprison them, and so together, weighted by the burden of sadness, Auntie and Scarlett trudged out of the butcher's shop and all the way out of the little village.

CHAPTER 12

The City and the Lake

Maya was thrown onto the grey beach. The wind howled, and voices and sirens crashed in the distance. When was she? There was only one way to find out. Still unsettled from her narrow escape from the village, she willed herself out of the beach and into whatever lay beyond.

She emerged in the midst of a cacophony of noises. Cars honked and swerved aggressively on a burning-hot asphalt street. The air was filled with the stench of pollution and the general din of a city. She looked around in wonder.

Fifty-story buildings glared down at her from every direction, their windows glinting maliciously in the bright sunlight, but she didn't mind. She began to walk down a pale cement sidewalk. People bustled around her muttering "Excuse me" as they pulled their briefcases close and went back to talking on the phone. The city couldn't have been more different than the small village with the knights. The humans here paid her no attention to her whatsoever, dismissing her as part of the background. She loved it.

There was a vibrancy here, a colorful feeling in the air, which buzzed with life and activity. It resonated within her, and she found herself smiling.

She strolled down street after street, gazing enchantedly at the supermarkets and corner stores she passed, at every restaurant and café. It felt as though she walked for miles, and yet she never tired. The sun was smiling and the sky was a charming forget-me-not blue. Small breezes rushed through intersections and down wide boulevards, just as busy as the people.

There was so much to see, so much to learn. The specks of gold and silver in her eyes danced delightedly as the force of so many lives beat a steady drum in her ear.

Slowly, she made her way out of the city center to a neighborhood with small brick buildings. Families laughed, grinning broadly, emanating waves of care and community. Kids played tag in the street and jumped off the front stoops of their buildings while parents issued half-hearted warnings and talked with other couples. These were kids just like her; they were her age, and yet their lives were so different, she thought.

These kids all lived on top of each other in apartments, not in separate houses like the People of the Land. They were in this fabulous city where they could explore and carve their own way in life. Maya felt a pang followed by an irresistible longing, like she was a magnet being drawn to those tall, formidable buildings.

Overwhelmed by sudden exhaustion, she slumped down on a stoop. She had just realized she had found a place she loved more than the Land of the Clouds, more than her home. And she thought she finally understood what drove her parents away from the Land and to Earth—a sense of freedom that only Earth could possess. With this thought in her head, she felt her eyelids close, and she drifted off into a heavy sleep.

When she awoke, it was night. A streetlight near her glowered, chiding her for falling asleep. She looked around. Her eyes were not yet fully open, and she could only make out the bleary outlines of dark shapes around her. She rubbed her face with her fists and gazed around again. The apartment buildings around her were hidden in shadows, and a faint orange haze tinged the indigo sky, causing the stars to fade away. She scowled. Pollution.

She stood up and rummaged in her pack for something to eat. Chewing on a granola bar, she contemplated the state of her adventure. She vaguely recalled thinking that she liked Earth better than the Land before she'd fallen asleep. And she did love Earth, loved its endless possibilities. But—she was the one in the prophecy. She *needed* to find 15 Harding Street.

The choice seemed to weigh down on her shoulders. Earth? The prophecy? Earth? The prophecy? Surely the prophecy, going to 15 Harding Street was more *important*...

Maya just couldn't bring herself to go to Harding Street quite yet, though. She wanted to enjoy Earth for a little longer.

She thought for another moment and then came up with a plan. She would go to one or two more places on Earth and then to 15 Harding Street. After all, Harding Street wasn't going anywhere, and if she did them in the opposite order, she might be so busy fighting the OCT—or doing whatever the prophecy required—that she might forget to finish her travels on Earth.

She promptly decided that, seeing as it was dark out, now was the perfect moment to time travel. This time she could choose her destination a little more carefully, she thought, although ending up in the city had proven to be an excellent accident. She concentrated, willing herself to descend to the grey beach.

It was harder this time; it was as if the beach were trying to force her back onto the street. She gritted her teeth and focused even harder. Slowly but surely, she began to enter the grey beach. The force was still pushing her out, but she was able to overcome it.

She was thoroughly tired now, although she was only standing on the beach. The amount of energy she was using was equal to that of focusing on the head of a pin and willing it to explode. Sweat pouring down her face, she stepped forward into the waves. The ocean was colder than she remembered, and the icy water immediately seeped far inside her body. She shivered. The waves were also rockier, crashing loudly on the beach, spraying water high in the air.

She took another step, and then another. She could still hear the sounds of the street in the city, now punctuated with running footsteps and cries of "Closer, closer."

She nearly lost her footing on the slippery sand. *Closer, closer?* What was that about? Did someone know about her? No, she was just being paranoid, Maya told herself, forcing herself to go knee deep in the water.

She had now reached the end of the sandbar, she knew, and it was time to dive in. She could barely bring herself to. She was shivering madly, and she felt dizzy and dehydrated. Nevertheless, she pushed onward, diving into the frigid water.

She swam dutifully on, the water seeming to rush into her head, befuddling her senses, whispering, hissing nonsensically in her ear. She closed her eyes, then opened them and saw the Tunnel of Time stretching down below her. She recalled her previous two journeys here. The first time she had been ecstatic, elated at finding the tunnel. The second time she had been in a rush, desperate to get away from the butcher and sheriff. Now she felt dead, as if her body had long given up on trying to move. The tunnel brought her no joy, no thrill of excitement. It was merely a means to get out of this torturous state.

Maya swam through the tunnel, watching the scenes in the waves without much conviction. A heavy weight was pulling her down, down, and she didn't care enough to stop it. One scene caught her eye. It seemed to be very far back in time. A small lake filled the valley where the village and the city had been. *I've never seen a lake*, thought the one part of her that could still think coherently. *Let's go there.*

There was no argument from the rest of her body, which saw any scene as a release from this prison. With a great effort, she pushed through the scene. It split in half, and the rush of water propelled her forward.

She went limp as she raced through the ocean. The water was carrying her, and she saw no reason not to sit back and relax. Her limbs ached terribly, and it felt as though fireworks were going off in her head and in front of her eyes.

Finally, she arrived at the grey beach, falling over, unable to keep her balance. Numbly, she stood up and, closing her eyes and tensing her body although it hurt, she willed herself into the scene with the lake.

She felt the warm sun on her face and cool grass soaking into her skin. Sighing and opening her eyes, she saw she was collapsed on a patch of grass. She rubbed her face and sat up—or, well, tried to. Her back strongly protested the movement and she fell back onto the ground, resolving to stay there until she felt a little better.

She stared up at the sky. It was a pale blue with scattered light-grey clouds. She smiled faintly. She had decided she loved the way the sky looked from Earth, loved the addition of clouds. And to think that, disguised in those grey wisps, there was a whole other society, completely hidden from humans...

The air was thick and moist, settling heavily on her skin, and as she lay there, her arms and legs limp, turning her head to stare alternately at the sky and the lake, she saw the day begin to change.

The lake, which had first appeared to be a dazzling blue with the reflections of clouds floating serenely across its surface was now grey and opaque, and the sky had become clouded. The air was cooler, though there was no wind. She had closed her eyes, on the brink of sleep, imagining how nice it would feel to jump in the lake, when the first droplets fell.

They were cool and hard. She opened her eyes and squinted up at the sky. The clouds had become a swirling collage of dark grey, like a tornado in the sky.

More drops fell, faster and faster. She let them slide down her face, relishing the way they dripped off her chin. She had never seen rain before. It felt nice, cleansing. She sat up, letting the beads of water sink into her hair. Leaving her backpack on the sodden grass, she carefully began to rise. Only a few seconds later, she stood in her soaked-through shoes, staring up at the rain.

She didn't mind that the rain hammered down on her, covering her skin and turning it glassy and reflective. She adored the way it felt, so powerful and strong. It was yet another of the wonders of Earth she had never experienced before. And again she had that feeling, slightly uncomfortable but sweet like candy, that she almost loved Earth more than the sky.

Everything seemed to be in greater detail here— finer, more enhanced. The colors were more vibrant, the scenery more splendid . . . and she was free. Here, she could do whatever she wanted. She had proven herself. No one had come looking for her yet. She had never felt more refreshed, more at home than now, as she jumped and twirled around the lakeshore, laughing delightedly at the Earth, at the warm embrace it wrapped her in.

Still, though, there was something missing, something that poked her in the back. Something she was unable to get ahold of.

The sky darkened even further until it might as well have been night. The air was thick and heavy, and yet when she laughed, she could hear it echo for miles. But something was off. The temperature was dropping faster and faster. Aches returned to her arms and legs, and she shivered in the cold. Kneeling down on the frozen grass, she pulled her cloak out of her bag and wrapped it around her shoulders, savoring the warmth it brought. Suddenly, a lightning strike gashed through the sky, tearing it open, releasing frozen rain and hail.

Maya's jaw trembled and her eyes held a cornered, scared look. She suddenly could no longer discern between present and past, between this day on the lakeside and that day eleven years ago when the sky had grown dark, when the figures had appeared. She whimpered in anguish, for she had heard something, a laugh booming over the hills, and she didn't know whether it was in her mind or not.

It was real, she thought. It was coming from just over the crest. Someone was after her, but who? Who could be after her?

Alone on the side of the lake, quivering under her cloak, she set about thinking. It wasn't hard to find the answer. She had come here, foolishly ventured to Earth, because she thought she was the one in the prophecy. The one in the prophecy. The thought rang in her head, jarring and sharp. And suddenly the spell that had been holding her captive, the sweetness of Earth, snapped.

What had she been doing? She had gotten distracted, sidetracked by the false promises of Earth. How could Earth ever be safe, be lovely? It was home to the OCT, the ones who had stolen her mother and father.

Maya stood up. She couldn't stay here. She had to go. Her mind was a whirlwind of bad plans. She needed to get to Shellside, UK. She knew that. This was a mission, she realized, fingering her necklace delicately, not a vacation on Earth. She had not proven herself yet. The prophecy—

that was how she would prove herself.

A pit of rage boiled in her stomach. How dare Earth capture her like this? How dare it hold her back from fulfilling her destiny? It was no better than the Land of the Clouds. Her nostrils flared, and she spit on the ground.

She heard the laugh again. It jarred her to the core. *I need to leave. Now. Where? Where?*

The answer fell on her like a bucket of ice. As little as she wanted to go back, she had to. She had to go back to the city—the place where she had really fallen in love with Earth, the place where, she realized now, she had become distracted from her mission. She needed to return, though. The city was sure to have methods of transportation that would get her swiftly over the channel that separated France from England.

Dreading her arrival back in that bustling hub, Maya began to concentrate, forcing herself from the lakeside and into the grey beach.

CHAPTER 13

Chasing Dreams

Scarlett and Aunt Flora, their heads hanging with disappointment, decided it would be best if they entered the forest next to where the knights were jousting before they time-traveled away.

"Where are we even going?" Scarlett asked sullenly.

"Away, I guess. I don't know. But there's nothing for us here, that's for sure." Auntie could feel wrinkles creasing her face. Sure, it had been a long shot to think that they would actually catch Maya on the first try, but still . . .

And what was Maya doing anyway? Auntie wondered as she and Scarlett entered the tangle of trees, surrounded by sweet, earthy air. Was she going to the address on her necklace? Or was she just taking a vacation on Earth? Based on the fact that Maya had clearly been in the medieval village, Auntie strongly suspected the latter. This made her sigh loudly. Maya was highly susceptible to being sidetracked.

Scarlett coughed quietly. Auntie realized she had been staring up at the canopy of branches and leaves, and she quickly turned toward Scarlett. "What?"

Her voice must have been harsh, for Scarlett looked somewhat taken aback.

"I just . . . I mean, we should probably get going, right? You yourself said that we can only catch Maya when her 'present-self' is actually there."

"Oh, yeah. Of course." It was Auntie's turn to look startled. Scarlett was right. They did need to get going. "But I don't suppose you can do that dream thing on command."

Scarlett shook her head. "Sorry."

Auntie tried to hide the disappointment that was being drawn on her face. "That's okay. I wouldn't expect you to . . ." Her voice trailed off. The two of them stood there, an awkward silence between them.

"But," Scarlett said suddenly, "if you give me Maya's dagger—assuming that's what triggered my dream last time—I can use it to see where she is."

"Oh!"

Gingerly, careful not to drop it, Auntie pulled the dagger out of her bag and gave it to Scarlett, who inspected it, turning it over on her palm. Then, the dagger still clasped in her hands, she closed her eyes.

Auntie watched Scarlett as her eyes fluttered beneath her lids. Scarlett went rigid as a board, then loosened, a coil of rope being spread out. Auntie's heart raced. Then after a few moments, Scarlett opened her eyes.

Auntie looked eagerly into Scarlett's eyes, as if expecting to see an image burned there. "Did you see her?" she asked.

Scarlett nodded, setting the dagger on the ground and then sitting down. She pulled her canteen from her bag and took a drink of water. "I saw her. She was in a city. A big city. She was getting ready to time travel—she was time traveling."

"When do you think it was?"

"Twenty-first century, I think . . ."

"So she's already gone from the city, then." Auntie looked forlorn.

Scarlett sighed. "Probably. But I saw more." Auntie perked up. "As Maya was disappearing, I saw a hill and a lake. I think she's going there next."

Auntie allowed a small smile to permeate the worry on her face. "So we'll go there. Our last stop. This time, I'm sure we'll catch her, and then we can take her home."

Scarlett hesitated. "There's one more thing."

"What?"

"I think there are people after Maya. Chasing her. I saw two men, and they seemed like they were looking for her."

Auntie frowned, foreboding filling her stomach. "And they weren't the police from the Land? I mean, they promised they wouldn't come searching on Earth, but maybe . . ." She trailed off as Scarlett shook her head.

"No. These weren't the police. They were . . . bad. I could just feel it. And they seemed really angry at not finding her too." She paused. "I'm worried."

Auntie didn't respond.

They stood in silence, listening to the wind rustling the leaves and the birds chirping. How could the world be so pretty when Maya was in danger?

After a few minutes, Auntie spoke.

"So Maya's going to this lake, right?"

"Right."

"Well, then we'd better get going."

"Right."

Scarlett could hardly say more than that. The full effect of the situation had hit her, smashed into her like a bullet train. There were people, dangerous people, looking to hurt, possibly to kill, her best friend. And she, Scarlett, was one of the only people who could save her. Her pulse beat fast and loud in her chest, in every part of her body. She looked over to Auntie. Her eyes were closed, and she was beginning to fade.

Scarlett tried to cast her worrisome thoughts away. She focused on entering the rainy street, on approaching the slate building. And there she was. On the street. Heavy raindrops fell on her head, splattering the ground with shimmering water. Scarlett made to step forward through the thick air, but something felt different.

It was hard to move. There was a beat resounding through the air, a *DA-DUM, DA-DUM* that sent tremors through her skin. She knew all too well that it was the sound of her own heart. *This wasn't supposed to happen*, she thought. *It shouldn't*. And the air, it was choking Scarlett, pouring in through her nose and mouth, constricting her lungs. It expanded inside her, suffocating her. Tears filled her eyes. What was happening?

She let all of her attention go, let it fly away, and suddenly she was back on the forest floor, tired and aching, though no longer dying. Scarlett tasted the salty tears splashing down her face. She couldn't time travel. For whatever reason, she couldn't. She was stuck here.

Scarlett looked around. Auntie was just barely visible, her image almost entirely wiped away. "Flora!" Scarlett yelled in desperation, her voice cracking. "Flora! Help me!"

Her voice must have penetrated to the world Auntie was in, for her outline became clearer and clearer, and suddenly she was standing over Scarlett, looking vaguely annoyed and frustrated. "What?"

"I can't time travel," Scarlett sobbed, covering her face with her hands.

Auntie's face melted. "What happened?"

"I just couldn't do it. It kicked me out." Scarlett wiped her runny nose on her sleeve.

Auntie sighed. "That can happen. Especially when you're young. It can be very harmful." *Is it going to happen to Maya?* Scarlett wondered.

"You'll be okay though . . . and you can simply time travel with me. It'll be a bit more work for me, but I'll be able to do it. I've time traveled with several people before."

Scarlett was amazed. "You can do that?" She had never considered the possibility of entering someone else's world.

"Yes," Auntie replied. "Hold onto my sleeve. Let's go."

Scarlett clutched the soft fabric of Auntie's sleeve tightly. "I'm ready," she croaked. Auntie closed her eyes and concentrated, lowering herself into her world and pulling Scarlett with her.

They appeared in a meadow. It was dry and arid, the type of place where merely breathing makes one's throat parched, and the grass, flowers, sky, and clouds were faded and greyish. Auntie strode with purpose toward the edge of the meadow, where the grasses grew taller and taller until they reached far over her head. Scarlett jogged along beside her, her fingers still curled around Auntie's sleeve. They walked fluidly through the grasses, wending random paths until Auntie exhaled a small puff of breath. The grasses in front of them parted. Scarlett gasped.

A hedge maze had been revealed. They stood at the entrance, a forking path ahead. The left path led out of the tunnel. The other curved and disappeared, weaving its way to the center of the maze. Auntie, without a moment's thought, took the right turn.

As they walked down the path, scenes appeared on the hedges. The Tunnel of Time. She and Auntie walked and walked through the stiff, silent air, past the same images that Scarlett had seen in her spiral staircase.

After a while, Scarlett saw the scene with the lake in the background. She tugged on Auntie's sleeve, but Auntie had already stopped. Without their movement, the hedge maze seemed to become even more quiet. Then Auntie parted the hedges in front of them, splitting the scene in half.

A wind carried Scarlett and Auntie over the tall grasses , which were prickly and sharp, poking Scarlett in the back. Finally, the wind ceased and dumped the two of them back in the meadow.

As Auntie concentrated on lifting them back to Earth, Scarlett let everything she had seen sink in. It was so strange to be in someone else's world. She felt like she was trespassing, like she wasn't allowed. It had been almost ghostly, she decided, as she and Auntie emerged by the lake. Scarlett let go of Auntie's sleeve, and she flexed her hand, trying to coax her white knuckles back to normal.

Compared to the meadow, the hill was bursting with sound. Every lap of water from the lake seemed noisy and every footstep on the soft grass overly loud. Scarlett looked around. The sky was clouded and rain was pouring down. Scarlett pulled a cloak out of her backpack and covered herself.

"Are you okay?" Auntie called over the rain.

Scarlett nodded.

"Where is she?" Auntie scanned the valley and the lake below for as far as she could see, panic creeping into her voice. "You said she was by the lake."

"She was," Scarlett hollered back, her voice rough with fear. "I'll go down and look. I'm sure she's here."

Scarlett, keeping her cloak wrapped tightly around herself, began the treacherous descent down the slippery hill. It was hailing now, balls of ice pelting her. Then an evil laugh came from Auntie's direction and Scarlett slowed for a moment, torn. Help Auntie or save Maya? In her moment of indecision, she tripped and rolled down the hill, the wet grass slapping her face without mercy. She landed close to the lake, close to where Maya should be. Scarlett's heart was pounding; she was close, so close.

The laugh rang out again, but Scarlett didn't look back this time. Aunt Flora could handle herself.

Scarlett stumbled to the edge of the lake and squinted,

staring down the shore, waiting for a small figure to break the grey air. And she saw her: just a glimpse of a cloak, vanishing. "Maya!" Scarlett screeched, her stomach flipping around. But her friend was already gone.

Scarlett could have stood there forever in the soaking rain, chilled to the bone, watching the spot where Maya had been. She had been so close, just over seven feet away. And yet …

A hand shook Scarlett's shoulder. She whirled around and saw Auntie, face white and pale. Her arm was bleeding slightly. "We need to go." Her tone was urgent, her blue eyes wild.

"What—" Scarlett asked, shivering, her brow furrowed.

"Now!" Auntie yelled, close to breaking. "Hold on!"

Scarlett gripped her sleeve once more, and they slipped away into the faded meadow.

CHAPTER 14

The Last Adventure

At the grey beach, the ocean was turbulent and violent; it seemed as though a hurricane was about to strike. Barely able to keep her eyes open, Maya stepped wearily into the water. Knee-deep in the frigid waves, she slumped over, remembering the rain on the hill and how refreshing it had felt. How natural, how real . . .

Then she snarled, her nostrils flaring. How had she allowed the beauty of Earth to lull her into a false sense of security? A fire roared in her stomach, giving her the energy to dive into the water.

Hardly aware of her surroundings, she swam deep into the rolling ocean. *Almost there,* she told herself. *Almost at 15 Harding Street. Almost ready to fulfill the prophecy.*

When the tunnel appeared before her, she thought her brain seemed to be delayed; by the time she realized she had seen the city, she was already past it. With immense effort, she turned around and pushed herself through the scene.

She emerged near the stoop where she had slept. It was dawn, but cars still rushed by, buildings were alight, and people strolled down the streets. The sky was a smudge of lightening indigo infused with a toxic orange, the color of light pollution. But the air, it was crisp and fresh, wafting down sidewalks on puffs of early morning breeze, just like in the Land of the Clouds.

Maya leaned against the cold brick wall of an apartment building. She closed her eyes and imagined the Land. She had hardly ever woken up far before dawn— that was Auntie's pastime—but on the occasions she had, she remembered the air being still and silent, asleep. It was a new world at the beginning of each day.

Hastily, she wrenched her eyes open and wiped away the tears that had formed. This was not the time to be sentimental, she told herself. This was the time to get out of the city.

Her bag slung over her shoulders, she began stumbling down the street, tripping over nonexistent roots and divots in the sidewalk. She was looking for a subway or a train or something like that, she knew: in school in the Land, they had been taught about human transportation.

She sleepily inspected every street corner she came to, searching for a staircase or a sign bearing the name of a station. About ten blocks down, she saw a small group of people emerging from an escalator leading into the ground. Heart thumping, she strode over, trying to seem cool and nonchalant instead of nervous and exhausted.

She stepped onto the escalator and gripped the railing tightly as it descended. She awkwardly stepped off at the bottom and looked around. The light was fluorescent, prying, its harsh whiteness leaving no shadows. The walls, she noticed as she walked toward the ticket barrier, were a grimy white tile coated with years of dirt.

There were hardly any people in front of the chrome turnstiles, except for a few commuters and one bored-looking guard in his booth, who was watching the passersby with an idle expression.

Trying to appear perfectly comfortable and normal, she stepped up to a turnstile, subtly glancing at the man next to her to see what he was doing. The man inserted a plastic card into a slot. The slot spit the card back out and the turnstiles opened. The man walked through.

She was beginning to get worried—she didn't have a card. She looked around. There were three people riding down the escalator into the station, but they weren't paying her any attention, and the guard was lazily watching a grubby spot on the wall, chewing absently on the cuff of his jacket.

She took her chance. Attempting to control the rapid pulse of her heart, she ducked under the turnstile, crawling on the sticky, smelly cement floor. She stood up and wiped her hands, waiting for sirens to go off, for the guard to yell at her. But nothing happened. The only noises were the distant honks and screeches as trains pulled into their platforms.

Nearby, a map of the subway was bolted to the wall. She rushed over. Her anxiety over climbing under the turnstile seemed to have neutralized her fatigue for the time being, and she felt spry and energetic.

A large sign was plastered next to the map of the subway. *Rue du Monet*. It was on the Red Line, only five stops away from *Station Principal*, which seemed to be large, for it was represented by a big dot on the interweaving web of stations. From there, she figured she could maybe get on a train that would take her at least to the Channel, if not under it.

She hurried down a corridor covered with brightly colored movie posters and emerged on the platform. A few people lingered on the side of the platform, steering clear of the yellow tape right in front of the empty tracks. She ran up to it. She looked down. A few feet below her, black tracks stretched out, continuing all the way through ominous tunnels to her right and left. She was in awe; she had never seen anything so abrasive and impersonal.

A wind whistled through the tunnel. Something above her head blinked, and she looked up. There was a screen above her head, displaying bright orange letters. *Next train*, it read in French, *will be arriving in less than a minute*. She felt herself grin. She was traveling on Earth. Like a real human. Like her parents. And she was on her way to 15 Harding Street.

CHAPTER 15

Followers

Scarlett and Auntie emerged in an empty field. The grass was cool and moist, and the nighttime sky was blanketed with dark grey clouds. The air was thick, but pleasantly so, not in an ominous, foreboding way.

Scarlett inhaled a shaky breath, still processing the events by the lake.

"Someone's definitely after her." Auntie's voice was soft, but it trembled as if it were about to tip over.

"Yes, they are," Scarlett said quietly.

"Where do we . . . *when* do we go next?"

"I don't know." Scarlett played with a piece of grass. "Listen, Flora. There's something I need to tell you."

Auntie looked up at Scarlett, pressing her hand over the gash on her arm. "What is it?" She seemed to have trouble forming the words.

Scarlett swallowed. "I saw her. I saw Maya."

"You—" Auntie did indeed begin to crumble, melting into specks of dust on the ground.

Scarlett nodded.

"Did you talk to her?" Her voice was hoarse and raspy as she clung to Scarlett's next words.

"No." The word sounded like lead. "She—she was just disappearing. I called out, but . . . then she was gone."

Auntie opened her eyes wide, blinking back tears. "Well. At least we know she's alive." The words "for now" dripped off the end of the sentence, though Auntie didn't dare to speak them.

"Yes. But Flora," Scarlett asked tentatively, "who are

the people after Maya?"

Auntie sighed heavily, wrapping a bandage around her arm. "I think they're probably from the OCT."

"So you think—"

"Maya might be the one in the prophecy. She herself certainly thinks so. And I don't think we can rule it out either."

"But then she's really in danger." The words sat in the air.

"Yes, she is. And we're the only ones who can help her."

Auntie lay down, staring up at the sky, one hand on her arm.

"What happened to your arm?" Scarlett enquired, still sitting up.

"One of the men on the hill. He had a sword." She sounded calm, as if it were no big deal. Scarlett let this sink in.

"Let's stay here for the night, catch up on some sleep," Auntie said. "In the morning we'll get going. Wherever, whenever we decide to go."

Scarlett nodded, though in the dark she didn't suppose Flora could see. "Good night then."

"Good night, Scarlett."

Scarlett lay down, wrapping herself in her cloak, and closed her eyes. She should've been tired—she should've been ready to collapse—but she wasn't. Was Maya really the one in the prophecy? It just seemed so incredible. And yet . . . Scarlett debated this point back and forth in her head until she finally fell into a restless sleep under the dark, dark clouds.

Scarlett woke up with a start. Her eyes darted around as she refamiliarized herself with her surroundings. Auntie was sitting up, applying salve to her wound. "What is it?"

"Another dream."

Auntie's blue eyes became more intense.

"She's going to the place on the necklace. 15 Harding St. Shellside, UK."

Auntie froze for a moment. And then she stood up, fast. "Let's go."

Scarlett got up as well and slung her bag over her shoulder.

"How is she traveling?"

"Train. She was in a big city, and she's taking a train to London."

"Train, train," Auntie muttered, pacing back and forth. "There's no faster way than that," she decreed, "unless we have time to book seats on a plane, which we don't." She paused. Scarlett was bewildered.

"Have you been to Earth before?" It was a question that had been percolating in the back of Scarlett's mind for a very long time.

"Yes, of course." Auntie looked taken aback. "I fought against the OCT, didn't I?"

"You did?" Scarlett exclaimed. "You've never mentioned that!"

"Yes, well . . . and then I had the same job as your mother. Fixing the small problems that the OCT caused on the Earth after the war."

Scarlett's eyes widened further.

"And," Auntie said, pulling something out of her bag, "that's why I know how to use this."

Scarlett squinted at the object. It was small and dark, and looked vaguely familiar. "What is it?"

"A teleporter. People like your mom use them when they are on Earth, so they can travel more quickly. I used to have one too. Anyway, the police in the Land lent me one before we came down here."

Scarlett was mildly confused. "But how does it work?"

"Well," Auntie said, "you can only travel about 400

yards with it at one time, but you move instantaneously. Now hold onto my sleeve. Let's go."

15 Harding Street

As the train rolled along through France, Maya sank into a daze. She was thoroughly exhausted, ready to collapse and sleep and only wake up when she felt all better. And yet she couldn't do that. Somewhere in the back of her mind, a voice was whispering to her: *You're so close. Just a little bit farther and you'll be there.* It was this urge that kept her eyes half open as she stared out at the blur of land.

The train whirred past houses and towns where people were playing outside, where the windows of houses were open to admit luscious summer breezes. She imagined how it would feel not to have a task weighing down upon herself, adding to the heaviness of fatigue. And yet she shouldered her burden with pride. It was her mission, and she was going to see it through.

She saw a girl galloping on a horse, spurring it onward, laughing and smiling while the sun splashed upon her face, and a few minutes later, lulled by the imaginary rock of the horse, she finally fell asleep.

It was a deep, complete sleep, with no dreams and no nightmares. Her head drooped against the window, rattling as the train forged onward, and she slept and slept and slept.

The sun was much lower in the sky when she awoke. It was as though she were rising from a warm bath; she was groggy but clean feeling. Wiping the sleep— the blessed sleep!—from her eyes, she looked out the window. The sun was touching the edge of a large field, lighting it ablaze with vibrant red, orange, yellow, pink, and purple. She sighed contentedly. She looked around her compartment, for she had never really observed her surroundings before falling asleep.

It was small, with only the bench where she was sitting, and then one across from it. A plastic table folded out between them. She ran her hand over the sleek surface, relishing its touch against her fingers. She gazed upward. A small light had flickered on as the sun sank outside.

A sliding glass door separated the compartment and the rest of the train. All she could see through the door was a narrow hallway adorned with windows. She presumed there was a bathroom—and perhaps some food—somewhere, but there was no sign of either from where she sat. Satisfied, she sank back in her seat and continued staring out the window.

A short while later, the sun had fully disappeared behind the horizon, leaving a beautiful, indigo-tinged sky in its wake. She could hardly see out the window anymore; only her reflection was visible as the evening grew darker. She pulled some fruit out of her bag and was nibbling contentedly on it when a loud ding echoed throughout the train. Her heart pounded. *Please*, she prayed. *Don't let it be anything bad.*

A crackly voice spoke over the speaker. "We will be arriving in London in approximately thirty minutes. Please be ready to exit the train upon arrival."

Maya felt her heart relax. She smoothed her silky, dark hair calmingly. Then she stopped. London? In thirty minutes? But that meant that the train was already in England... which meant... she was close to Shellside. Very close.

Auntie and Scarlett sat on a hillside in the dark. They had spent the whole day teleporting, and now... now they were in England. Near Shellside. The sun had set a little while earlier, but they had not moved. They were so close. *And yet*, Scarlett wondered, *what if something went wrong?*

Scarlett coughed. "Should we get going?"

"Probably. Maya'll be getting to Shellside in a few hours or so, I'd guess . . ." Auntie's voice trailed off.

"But?" Scarlett prompted, reading into the silence.

"Well, when we go to 15 Harding Street, we have to be sure to be there in the same time as Maya is."

"True," Scarlett admitted. Her heart was pounding now. "So, what are we going to do?"

"Wait."

Scarlett had stood up, ready to make their next move. "Wait?" she cried, the tension snapping her in half.

"Yes, wait. We can use your power on Maya's dagger and figure out which time period she's going to. We'll time travel and then teleport there . . ."

"How can you be so calm about this?" Scarlett demanded, her voice wavering.

"I'm not, Scarlett. I'm not." Auntie's eyes misted and tears formed at the corners. "I don't know what I'll do if I don't find her." Auntie seemed to be talking more to herself now. "At home, she could act out, she could get angry, but it was okay. I knew she was safe." Tears flowed down Auntie's face. "But here, she's gone in too deep. Time traveling again might be too much for her. We need—*I* need to find her." By the end, Auntie's voice was barely a whisper.

Scarlett swallowed. Awkwardly, she put her arm over Auntie's shoulder, wrapping her in an embrace. "We'll find her," she promised. "I'm sure we will."

Fighting off a new wave of exhaustion, Maya plopped down on a seat in the train bound for Cornwall. She was close to her goal, close to finding answers. She had done it, and beneath her heavy eyelids, she felt an extreme sense of pride well up inside. If only there was someone she could share it with. For a moment her thoughts drifted to Auntie. Auntie, who had raised her and cared for her. How had she reacted to Maya leaving? Then Maya shook the thought from her head. No. She would complete the prophecy, and then she would be able to go home and everyone would be proud of her. Yes, then everyone would be proud of her.

The six-hour journey passed slowly as molasses spilling out of a jar, until finally the train screeched to a halt. In just a few minutes, she would find out what had happened to her parents. She would find out everything; she was sure of it. She had to find out everything.

Tightly clutching her necklace, she staggered off the train. Although her mind was buzzing, her arms and legs felt as though they had been beaten with a wooden club.

She lurched across the platform toward a sign reading "Local Map," then set off into the lamplit night.

Eleven minutes later, Maya tottered down Main Street in Shellside. Her feet made soft echoes on the cement street, bounding into the still night. There was no one out. It was surreal. She could hardly believe that she was standing in Shellside, the place that had consumed her thoughts for the last several days, the place that was somehow connected to her parents.

Small buildings about three stories high lined the street. She glimpsed storefronts: displays of glass flowers, pens and pencils, women's dresses, sports balls, plates and dishes, and everything under the sun. It made her smile to see such a rich life, a life she felt she knew well, having now spent time on Earth. And there, at the end of Main Street, was a sign. She stopped in the middle of the street, wobbling, as a salty ocean breeze flew overhead. Harding

Street. There it was at last. She ran toward it, nearly tripping over her own unsteady feet.

When she turned the corner, though, she was faced with a chain-link fence and a bright-orange sign. "Demolition Site," she read in the harsh, cruel light from a streetlamp. "Please stay clear." Beyond the fence was a mountainous pile of rubble.

She sank down in the middle of the street. It was gone. She had come so far, and it was gone. All the excitement that had filled her body was replaced by a seeping, cold feeling.

She pulled off her necklace and stared at it, tears blurring her vision. How was she supposed to find her answers? How? How? As she looked up into the starry sky, into the underbellies of massive clouds, it came to her. She was from the Land of the Clouds. She could time travel. She would time travel. She *had* to. She needed to find a time in the past when Harding Street was alive and standing, when she could find the answers.

Refastening her necklace around her neck, she willed herself down to the grey beach.

There was a storm raging. A full-blown hurricane. It had finally arrived.

She was nearly swept off her feet by the force of the roaring wind, but by tensing every muscle in her body to the point where she thought they would snap, she managed to anchor herself.

Every step into the water was torture. Her limbs trembled frightfully, and the icy water was so frigid that it felt like lava. Swaying, about to pass out from the effort, she reached the end of the sandbar. Now came the hardest part: the swim.

The current slammed into her head like rocks being thrown down a mountain. Still, she pressed onward. She swam through the ocean, though with every passing second she felt closer to being utterly annihilated, and then blinked with difficulty. The Tunnel of Time appeared, swirling in the depths.

She swam down the tunnel, hating every minute she spent there. And then, finally, she saw it: a scene where Harding Street was bustling with people. She squinted at a newspaper stand on the sidewalk. "May 18, 2019," the date read in big, bold letters.

The year 2019. She didn't know much about 2019, only that at the end of that year, a coronavirus called COVID-19 had emerged, leading to a pandemic. But the streets were full, and no one was wearing a mask so . . . this must have been before COVID-19. Maya shrugged to herself. It seemed good enough. She plunged into the image.

Scarlett's eyes flew open; she was no longer in the black emptiness she saw when she used her power, but on the nighttime hillside next to Auntie, holding Maya's dagger.

"She's time traveling." Her voice was hollow.

"No . . ." Auntie muttered.

"She's going to May 18, 2019."

Auntie held out her arm. Scarlett grabbed her sleeve, and they descended into the faded meadow, racing to find May 18.

Maya pulled herself out of the grey beach with an effort that seemed to leave her empty inside. Harding Street was busy and loud, filled with people walking up and down the street and chatting with friends. Store doors opened and closed, emitting little jingles as they did so, while people streamed in and out.

She felt feeble and frail, hardly able to move. She

panted just from the effort of standing. And yet she was smiling, smiling as she never had before. She was here at Harding Street.

Pulling off her necklace—just so she could feel it in her palm—she stepped forward into the glistening sunlight. Nearby, there was a newspaper stand with a short man behind the counter. "May 18, 2019," his newspapers read. Maya almost laughed. Part of her had been worried she would somehow travel to the wrong time. But she hadn't.

As she hobbled out toward the street, she saw it: just across from her, over the tops of two cars shining in the sunlight, was 15 Harding Street. This time she did laugh. Still holding her necklace in her hand, she ran toward it as best she could.

It was a cute little storefront, with a light-blue awning and polished glass in the window that showed off cases of jewelry: shining necklaces, bracelets, and earrings.

She stood in the middle of the street staring at number 15, imagining what it would look like inside, imagining the answers she would find when she walked in. Just then, a bicycle careened down the street. She turned around to see it just as it slammed into her chest.

She didn't feel it hit her. She didn't feel anything. As if in slow motion she fell, her necklace clattering to the ground, and hit the hot asphalt with a thump.

———————————

Scarlett and Auntie stood at the intersection of Main and Harding, hearts pumping, waiting for a glimpse of Maya. A cyclist zoomed by.

After a minute, they turned down Harding Street. It was busy, full of happy humans, but as far as Auntie or Scarlett could see, none of them were Maya. And then something shiny caught Scarlett's eye. She sprinted into the middle of the street, Auntie trailing after her. Scarlett picked something up, turned it delicately over in her hands.

"What is it?" Auntie asked, breathing fast.

Scarlett placed the object in Auntie's hands. It was small and cool. Auntie looked down. It was Maya's necklace.

Scarlett couldn't move. She couldn't think. Maya never took off her necklace. And where was she? Realization came hailing down. Somehow Maya was gone, and she hadn't chosen to go. Tears poured down Scarlett's face.

Scarlett looked up at Auntie. Her face was just a blur to Scarlett through her tears, but she could see that Auntie was sobbing too. Their arms wrapped around each other, they walked to the edge of the street and cried and cried and cried.

Maya was falling, falling through darkness, through space.

She tried to will herself to the grey beach, but it didn't work. She couldn't make it work. She couldn't time travel. The grey beach was closed to her now.

She fell and fell, growing more tired as she did so. Just as her eyes closed, right before she fell straight into unconsciousness, three words popped, stark white, in front of her shut eyes: "WE ARE COMING."

Part Two

CHAPTER 1

The Third Beginning

Maya woke with a start in a dirty cobblestone alleyway with sooty buildings and a cloudy sky overhead.

Who's coming? she wondered vaguely, her mind hazy and clouded.

She turned slowly and reached out to stroke the side of a concrete building. Its touch was cool and firm, definitely real. How had she gotten here? But where was "here"?

She felt her head in the place where it had hit the ground back on Harding Street. There was nothing, not even a bruise. Given that she was one of the People of the Land, she wasn't too surprised. But usually it took a little longer than that for her to heal.

Her brow furrowed. She reached down to her chest, instinctively clutching the spot where her necklace lived. Then she cried out in astonishment and shock. It wasn't there. It. Wasn't. There.

The alleyway swam before her eyes. *How had it . . .? If it wasn't here . . .?* She thought frantically back to Harding St. *What—oh . . .*

She slumped against the sooty side of a building, her face downcast. She had taken the necklace off. She had taken her most prized possession off, and then, when she'd been hit by the bicycle, she had dropped it.

Tears sprang to her eyes, geysers preparing to burst. She had to have that necklace. She *needed* it.

Part of her knew it was gone forever, and her sorrow opened a hole inside her while another part refused to believe it, insisting on trying to cover up the hole, though these attempts failed as the hole expanded.

The part of her that could not believe the necklace was gone felt over her shoulder for her bag. Maybe it was there. Maybe she was remembering wrong. *Maybe ...*

But her hand only snagged the sleeve of her tunic. She froze, rigid, and then twisted around, trying to see her back, trying to see whether the bag was really gone too.

It was.

Her money, her food ...

She sat down against a building, wiped her runny nose on her sleeve, stared at the grey, foreign sky, and let the tears flow. She cried with her head buried in her arms, trying to summon the fading aroma of the house that she and Auntie shared in the Land of the Clouds.

She had been so foolish, so stupid, to believe she was the one in the prophecy. She was just a little kid, an eleven-year-old who wanted to believe that the world needed her. No one needed her. She doubted anyone could even find her, seeing as she herself had no clue where or when she was.

She had come to Earth on an impulse, on a whim, hoping to find answers. She had never had a plan. She had never known what she would find at the elusive 15 Harding Street. If she had been the one in the prophecy, she told herself, the one destined to defeat the OCT, the one who knew it was her fate to do so, she would've thought ahead. She would have been aware of her goal. She wouldn't have held onto the childish fantasy of seeing her parents again.

This last thought, this painful, sharp acknowledgement that she had secretly hoped to find her parents still alive, caused the tears to stream harder, faster, a violent river of emotion cascading from her eyes.

At last, when her eyes were red and puffy and no more sobs would come, when her sleeves were drenched with snot and salty tears, when the world yelled that she had had enough time to wallow, Maya looked up.

Her vision was blurry and it hurt to see, but she squinted and peered around. The sky was still as dirty, as distasteful as it had been before, only now it was tinged with a darkness, an ink that spread through the air. The buildings around her were now no more than black silhouettes, foreboding and ominous.

She heard the squeak of wheels a ways off and jerked her stiff neck to face the entrance of the alley. Someone was getting off a bike. She flinched involuntarily.

The person—a boy, she thought, based on the cap on his head—was unloading a ladder from the back of the bike. He set it out in front of a dark pole and climbing up the ladder, he lit a lamp. Orange flames flickered into being, dancing merrily, casting a warm puddle of light onto the street. An old streetlamp.

She slowly stood up, careful not to draw the boy's attention, though he was already riding away. Her legs shook as she put weight on them, but they did not ache in the way they previously had. In fact, she mused, she didn't feel as nasty, as close to dying, as she had in her earlier adventures. Energy seemed to be slowly dripping back into her system.

She took stock of her situation, biting her lip as she did so. She was stranded, alone in a city she didn't know, in who-knew-what time period, with no way to contact anyone from the Land. This thought still sent a pang through her body, but it felt considerably more bearable than it had before. Something had changed. Something was growing in the hole inside her ...

Encouraged by her newfound energy and hope, she decided to try time travelling again. She concentrated, willing herself to visit the grey beach. Slowly, it started coming into focus: she could make out the hazy outline of the water and could faintly make out the waves rocking the beach. The storm had died down. She was so close to entering the beach, to stepping into the water, when the wind, seeming to act of its own volition, smacked her in the face, pushing her away.

"Stop!" she tried to cry, but her voice was swallowed. The winds kept howling, and before she knew it, she was back in the dark alley, stumbling backward into a wall.

She shook her head, restraining the tears that welled in her eyes. She had just stopped drowning, found a way to float, to keep her head above water in this unfamiliar situation, and now there was a weight, a burden of failure, trying to push her down.

She took a deep breath, steeling herself. She would not let it take her. She would keep swimming, keep going until she found land. But first she needed direction. She had to know where she was going. And that meant figuring out where and when she was.

She began to walk down the alleyway toward the streetlamp. She stepped into its glow, feeling its warmth course through her. She wondered how she looked in the orange light—likely not as happyhappy, as whole, as she had in the Land of the Clouds ...

She looked around. *Left, or right?*

On a whim, though she supposed her whims weren't very trustworthy lately, she went right. Another intersection. Go right. Another. Another. Her feet carried her aimlessly around as she peered at the buildings, most of which were dark, their windows covered by curtains.

She needed to find a place that would have the date and location. Someplace where it wouldn't seem suspicious that she needed to know that.

The thought sustained her as she walked on and on, the air becoming cooler. Finally, after what felt like hours, by which point the sky had turned entirely dark, a suffocating color, Maya saw a white light spilling out onto the sidewalk from beneath a green awning that read "TOM'S MARKET." She ran toward it, pushing through the front door, and found herself in a small market. A man stood behind a counter at the back of the store, surrounded by shelves stocked with goods. Maya coughed to get his attention. "Excuse me?" She spoke English, since that was the language that the sign outside was in.

"Yes?" The cashier wore a polite, bored expression on his small face as he spoke, his words carrying a heavy British accent.

Maya adjusted her own speech accordingly. "Do you have a newspaper I could look at?" Really, she needed anything with the place and date.

The cashier looked suspicious. "Sure. Right over by the door."

She thanked him, smiled, and then walked back over to the door, where there was a rack of newspapers she had previously failed to notice. She grabbed the top one on the stack and scrutinized the cover.

The date was April 12, 1910.

1910? Maya clutched the newspaper rack for support. She was in 1910? Had she been in a more futuristic time, she might've been able to somehow use modern technology to contact the Land of the Clouds so she could go home, but in 1910? There was no way.

She sighed. She still didn't know where she was. As she scanned the page, though, her location soon became apparent: "A London newspaper ... In the city of London ... Here, in London ... The weather in London ..."

That settled it. She was in London in 1910, a few years before the First World War. Now, if she could only find a way to send a message to the Land ...

Maya stood there, oblivious to her surroundings, until someone coughed behind her. Startled, she whirled around. A policeman stood there, his eyes narrowed. "Hello," he said.

"Hi," Maya replied nervously. What did he want? Was he going to arrest her? Did he know that she wasn't from Earth? Paranoia overcoming her, she resisted the urge to explain that she wasn't the one in the prophecy, so if he was looking for her, she was the wrong person.

"Where are your parents, little girl?" He sounded reserved, as though he had bad news that he was waiting to tell.

"I don't—I mean—they're—" she sputtered hopelessly.

"What's your name?"

"Rose," Maya blurted.

"Well, Rose," the policeman said. "Come with me."

CHAPTER 2

The Police Station

The policeman took a firm hold of Maya's sleeve and dragged her out of the market. Her heart pounded as he led her through darkened, deserted streets.

Her lungs were full of air she longed to exhale, but her throat seemed to have tightened so that she could hardly breathe, much less ask the question she so desperately wanted to know: *Where are you taking me?*

Finally, after over ten minutes of loud silence from the policeman—the only sound was the scuffle of his boots on the cobblestones—she forced her mouth open and shoved the words out. The policeman looked at her, his face stony.

"Where am I taking you? Where do you think? The police station."

She would've stopped dead in her tracks, except the policeman was still pinching her sleeve, and still walking.

"Why—why are we going to the police station?" Maya croaked, feeling slightly lightheaded. "I haven't broken any rules, have I?"

The policeman laughed, but it was a harsh laugh, the sound of a blade being sharpened. "No, Rose, you haven't 'broken any rules.' But you're just a kid. And you're alone on the streets. We can't have that happening. It's bad for the city. Frankly," he added, "it's a good thing I was at the market or else I wouldn't have found you."

Nothing the policeman was saying was reassuring Maya. She was so consumed with worry it felt like someone was jabbing a stick into her ribs. She had never been caught before. And how did she know that the policeman *wasn't* evil, wasn't working for the person with the cold laugh, the one she had heard at the lake? She might not be the one in the prophecy—and every time she thought that, her stomach dropped—but someone had been chasing her.

She was wrenched from her thoughts when the policeman abruptly stopped walking. They were standing on what could've been a main street, had it not been filthy and empty and full of litter.

"Ah, here we are," he said, satisfied. A sign reading "London Police Department" hung in a grimy window, gaslights illuminating a room behind it. The policeman pulled a key from his pocket and inserted it into a rusty lock on an old door. There was a click as the door creaked open.

There was only one room that Maya could see, though there were about five doors leading out of it. A few chairs were scattered across the room in haphazard rows, though they were all empty. Several discarded newspapers rested on their wooden seats.

She looked down. The floor was stone, though its smart, dull-grey hue was completely hidden by layers of dirt and dust. She fought the urge to sneeze, to rid herself of this grubbiness, and settled for looking up at the ceiling, which, granted, was not in much better shape.

As she inspected the ceiling, noting the cobwebs and the swaying gas lamp, she twitched her head slightly. Not only was there a faint stench of something rotting wafting from behind one of the doors, but there was a quiet buzzing as well, of an unfindable source, which seemed to create an unscratchable itch in her head.

The policeman coughed, and Maya realized she was standing in the middle of the dingy room. The policeman, and another who was behind an unbalanced desk, were watching her. She turned to face them.

Both policemen were dressed in the same shabby

uniform, though their badges gleamed in the light. "So, you found her, Jones?" the new policeman asked. He was tall and thin, rather like a twig, with only patches of brown hair left on his scalp.

Jones, the policeman who had dragged Maya to the station, nodded. Maya looked him up and down, not having had the opportunity to do so previously. He was squatter, and kept scratching his red, puffy nose.

"Where's she going to go?" Jones asked, not taking his eyes off of Maya.

"Um, let's see." The twig man bent down over the desk, adopting the shape of a mutated tree branch. He pored over a piece of paper, and then another, and then another.

"Attleboro's," he said finally.

"How far's that?"

"Just a few blocks. But I'd wait till morning."

Jones snorted. "'Course I'm waiting till morning. I've got a family of my own to tend to, don't I?"

The other officer nodded timidly. "Right, right. Want me to watch her until tomorrow?"

"Nah. She won't do much harm."

"But there isn't anyone else here. She'll be all alone."

Maya's gaze flitted between the two men as they talked. She didn't know whether she wanted to stay here overnight or go to the mysterious Attleboro's, and she was afraid to ask what the latter was. A prison, maybe? But why would they wait to send her to a prison?

While she debated this point, the two men seemed to come to an agreement, and by the time she had emerged from her own head, both officers were heading to the front door.

The tall officer twisted the gaslight off, submerging the room into darkness. He sighed, and Maya heard him walking over to the front door, which Jones held open for him. "Are you sure we shouldn't leave her some food or anything?"

"She'll be fine. Let's go."

The door creaked shut behind them. She heard the rusty lock click closed and, through the front window, saw the two men walk away, leaving her alone in the dark.

She shuffled briefly about the room, searching for a chair that was still structurally sound, and finally collapsed in one. It squeaked and groaned; the noises seemed to penetrate the still, empty air.

Though she could hardly see anything, the doors on the walls seemed to loom in the darkness, surrounding her. What was behind them? She supposed, under different circumstances, she might want to go investigate them. But now, a throbbing sense of loneliness tugged at her every molecule. She was stuck here without any friends, without family, without her necklace, without a way to go back to the Land of the Clouds. Tears slipped from her eyes, so miserable and desolate was she. She longed to be back in the house with Auntie, having their occasional fights, but safe, cocooned in the protection of the Land.

Sighing, she tilted her head back and stared at the dark ceiling. Suppose one of the spiders in its corners came down to her . . . Her hollow body shuddered at the thought.

And so Maya whiled the night away, chilled with dread, glancing at the foreboding doors, hugging her knees and mindlessly watching the cobblestone street, until the darkened sky lightened, becoming a soft grey, still covered with impenetrable clouds.

Soon the night fell away, and about half an hour after her stomach started to grumble, she heard someone walking down the street. The twiglike officer was whistling quietly as he passed the front window and then unlocked the door and admitted himself to the still-dark station.

Without noticing Maya, who was still hunched on a chair, her muscles sore, he twisted the gaslight and struck a match against it. Flames whooshed into the fixture, spreading light across the room.

Other than a simple nod in her direction, he paid no attention to Maya, instead settling himself behind his desk and beginning to pore over some papers. A few minutes later, Jones arrived.

"Morning." He nodded gruffly to Twig Man. "Come with me," he ordered Maya.

Maya stood up cautiously. She couldn't tell what mood Jones was in—angry, or very angry.

The pair stormed out of the station—well, Jones stormed. Maya, shuffling behind, was glad to be rid of the station. Its dirty, dingy presence, with its cracked ceiling and mysterious doors, seemed to be a cloud hovering over her mind. Stepping into the city air was slightly freeing, for although it was polluted, it was fresher, warmer, and cleaner than the air in the station. She nearly gasped, relishing its sweetness.

Jones turned to her. "What was that?"

Maya's stomach flipped. "Nothing," she muttered.

"I see you're quieter than yesterday. Nice change."

In that moment, Maya wanted nothing more than to attack Jones and run away. And she should, shouldn't she? she thought. She knew she could survive by herself. And she didn't even know where she was being taken. And yet . . . if she ran, she knew that, without any money, she would be stuck in London. Maybe at Attleboro's—whatever that was—there would be someone who could help. So she gritted her teeth and continued walking beside Jones.

They walked down a few streets, turning right at an intersection, then left, then left again, until they were on something like a main boulevard. Maya's eyes lit up for what felt like the first time in a while at the human life all around them. People laughed and strode on the sidewalks arm in arm, hand in hand. They emerged from tall buildings whose walls and windows, though still dirty, appeared happy and lively in the light.

Jones and Maya were nearing a main intersection. Maya was excited; beyond the crossroads, she could see bright awnings and shops and her heart leapt at the thought of walking by them. But then Jones stopped. She nearly ran into him.

"Aren't we going across the street?" she asked nervously.

"Nope. Right down here," he said, smiling a mean smile.

He turned left, toward an alley off the boulevard. Taleo Place.

Maya peered down Taleo Place. It was long and skinny and grimy, with only a sliver of daylight cutting through the sooty roofs, the type of street you expect to be littered with cigarette butts and broken bottles.

Jones strode proudly forward into the alley, and Maya had no choice but to follow. Where was he taking her?

As they went further into the alley, it curved slightly, and they could no longer see the main boulevard. Maya felt claustrophobic, trapped. She stared at the walls surrounding her. The buildings seemed to be townhouses, single-family homes, though they were thin and dirty. Maya couldn't imagine why anyone would choose to live here.

A small breeze rushed through the alleyway, and Maya shivered.

The alley seemed to turn once again. They passed numbers 20, 27, 31, 38, 46, 49—she frowned at the erratic numbering—and then they had reached the end. The end. It was a dead end. What was he going to—?

And then she saw it. A wooden sign, hand painted,

hanging next to the door of Number 50 Taleo Place. Mrs. Attleboro's Orphanage for Abandoned Children. That must be where he was taking her.

Abandoned children. Was that what she was, Maya thought. An abandoned child? She looked at the building that she would be living in. It was like all the others on the street: not particularly friendly looking. But the windows were scrubbed clean, unlike the others on Taleo Place.

Jones went up the stairs and stood on the front stoop. He knocked on the door, then faced her and gestured for her to join him.

A few seconds later, she heard the creak of someone turning the doorknob. After the person inside yanked on the door a few times, it was finally wrenched open. A small old woman stood on the threshold, her posture erect, her grey hair tied neatly back in a bun. Her sharp brown eyes flitted from Jones to Maya and back again.

"Mrs. Attleboro," Jones proclaimed, giving a little bow, "I've got another one for you."

CHAPTER 3

Mrs. Attleboro's Orphanage for Abandoned Children

Mrs. Attleboro thanked Jones and ushered Maya inside. "Come on, come on," she said, her tone as clipped as her gait, as she walked down a darkened hallway, leaving Maya to hurry after her.

Maya gazed at her surroundings as she walked, conflicted. Part of her hated being here and wanted nothing more than to be free, not constrained by a shabby little townhouse. But, she reminded herself, at least she would be around others. Plus, some rules would be good for her after her random wanderings through time. And after a little bit, maybe she would even feel better about not being the one in the prophecy, about being disconnected from everything she knew . . .

Maya looked up. The soles of Mrs. Attleboro's shoes had stopped clacking, and she was standing in front of a wooden door, bearing a sign that said "Office."

"Please come in."

Dust sparkled in the air, whooshing around as Mrs. Attleboro took a seat behind a polished wooden desk.

Mrs. Attleboro reached for a pen and a large leather notebook. Without looking at Maya, she leafed through its pages. Maya, peering over at the notebook, saw rows upon rows of names written in a delicate script, accompanied by columns of numbers and a few hastily written sentences.

Finally, Mrs. Attleboro sat back and flicked her chin up to look Maya in the eye. "Welcome," she said. Her tone was neither friendly nor cold, but responsible, like a pair of clippers pruning a bush in a garden. "I am Mrs. Attleboro.

And who might you be?"

"Um," Maya said, choking on the sound. "Rose."

"Rose who?"

"I—I don't have a family name." As she said it, she realized it was true. She had taken Auntie's name but never knew what her parents had been called.

"Ah, I see." Mrs. Attleboro sounded mildly disappointed as she wrote something down in the notebook.

"Now, Rose. As you know, you are in an orphanage. A place where children without parents live."

Maya nodded.

"I would like to ask you some questions about your past. Is that alright?" The sentence was phrased as a question, but there was no doubt that it was an order. Maya swallowed and nodded once more.

"Excellent." Mrs. Attleboro's fountain pen hovered over the yellowed notebook paper. "How old are you? Or, if you're not sure, how old do you think you are?"

"I'm eleven."

"Do you know when your birthday is?"

"February 1."

"Have you ever been in a home like this before?"

Maya shook her head, relieved that, so far, she could tell the truth.

"So, then, what did your upbringing consist of?"

"Sorry?" Maya tilted her head, confused. Her stomach squirmed.

"You said you are eleven. What have those eleven years of your life been like? Where did you live?"

"Oh, yeah. Well, I . . . mostly on the streets." Maya prayed that Mrs. Attleboro couldn't tell that her heart was beating rapidly.

Mrs. Attleboro watched Maya for a second as Maya tried very hard not to fidget. "I see . . . well, I suppose those are really the only things I need to know."

Maya's shoulders wanted to slump with relief, but she remained standing straight.

"Now, about living in this orphanage," Mrs. Attleboro continued. "I run this place. I take in anyone who comes to our front door, but there are certain standards everyone must uphold." This sounded like the beginning of a recitation Mrs. Attleboro had performed many times before.

"First and foremost, I must say that you are incredibly lucky that Officer Jones has brought you here and nowhere else. Out of all the children's homes in London, we are undoubtedly the most well kept. You will be treated well here, much better than you would be elsewhere.

"The rules. You will live here until either your eighteenth birthday or until a family offers to take you in. If you attempt to run away, you will be permitted to return here, but you may find that my demeanor will not be quite so pleasing then."

Maya fought the urge to smile. She didn't find Mrs. Attleboro's present demeanor very pleasing *now*.

"This orphanage," Mrs. Attleboro continued, "occupies two buildings. This one and the one across the street. This is the girls' building, where you will sleep, eat your meals, and have your classes. There is no circumstance under which you should enter the building across the street. That is the boys' building, which is supervised by my son, Mr. Attleboro.

"Your clothes"—Mrs. Attleboro looked up and down at Maya—"are undoubtedly of nice quality. You will be allowed to keep them, as well as any other possessions you might have, but you must wear our uniform. If you do not know how to sew, I'm sure one of the older girls can teach you. Does this all make sense, Rose?"

Maya nodded vaguely. She felt like she was floating, like everything around her was surreal, simply shapes made of mist.

"Excellent. Oh, and you will call me 'ma'am.'" Mrs. Attleboro's naturally sharp voice jarred Maya back to reality and she blinked, recalibrating.

"Yes, ma'am."

"Good." Mrs. Attleboro stood and strode over to her office door. Maya watched her as she peered out into the hallway. "Laila," she called. "Come here, please."

There was a scuffle of shoes coming down a creaky staircase, and then walking quickly over the paneled floors, a teenage girl appeared in the office doorway. "Here, ma'am."

"Thank you." Mrs. Attleboro gestured for Maya to stand and join her. "Rose, this is Laila. Laila, this is Rose, our newest ward."

Laila smiled, showing a large gap between her front teeth. "Pleased to meet you."

Maya flashed a grin as well, suddenly aware of how straight and perfect her own teeth were. Would she stand out? "You too," she mumbled.

"Rose, Laila is going to show you around the home and get you settled, alright?"

"Yes, ma'am." Maya was back to feeling like she was floating.

"Off you go."

"Come on," Laila said.

Together they went back down the darkened hall toward the front door. "So," Laila exclaimed, "this is the front hall. As you know, if you walk down the hall, you'll get to Mrs. Attleboro's office."

"Right, yes." Maya's tongue was burning with questions, even in her floating state. She wanted to ask about everything—Mrs. Attleboro's past, why the orphanage was at the end of Taleo Place, why . . .

Wait, she told herself, turning the word into a sort of chant, forcing her tongue to cool, forcing her questions back down her throat. *Wait. You'll find out later.*

To the right of the front door was another door. "This is our dining room," Laila said, leaning on the door to push it open. "And you'll notice that most of the doors around here are quite sticky. You'll usually need to shove them open."

The dining room was bigger than Mrs. Attleboro's office. It seemed to take up the whole depth of the building, for it had windows facing Taleo Place as well as the strip of dying grass out back. Four wooden tables were lined up in neat rows, two by two. Each table had six chairs, which were neatly pushed in.

Laila stood by the door while Maya walked around the room, feeling the grain of the tables. She was in front of one of the back windows, craning her neck to see a slit of grey sky above the dying grass, when a chime sounded: one, two, three, four . . . eight times altogether. Its echo resounded throughout the house. Maya flinched and looked back at Laila, who seemed entirely unsurprised. "What was that?"

"The grandfather clock in the study. It goes off every hour."

"Every hour?"

"Yep. Although at night, when all the doors are closed, you can barely hear it."

"Oh, okay."

There was a rumbling above them. Maya's gaze flicked upward. "And that?"

"The clock signals the change of classes. Everyone's just coming downstairs for class now."

When Maya looked perplexed, Laila added, "It's all part of our schedule."

"Oh.

"We get up at 6:00, although every few days, we have to get up earlier. We take turns making breakfast in the basement kitchen, and we eat at 6:15. Then there's some clean-up and studies start at 8:00."

Maya nodded meekly.

"Let's go. I've more to show you."

They went back out into the front hall, crossing to the door on the left side of the entrance. This is where we have our classes," Laila said quietly before pushing open the door.

Inside, Maya could see the neatly plaited heads of at least twenty girls, plus a few more heads with short hair.

She opened her mouth, but Laila answered her question before she could ask it. "Some of the boys do study with us. But most study in their own building."

Folding screens partitioned the space into three smaller rooms, each furnished with a few tables and chairs. One of the boys seated at a table nearby looked up, evidently having heard Laila's voice. He looked to be about Maya's age, with a broad face and rowdy, fire-orange hair. He grinned, and his eyes twinkled.

Laila scowled in return, her face adopting a disgusted expression. She turned around and stomped out of the room, though she was careful not to let her feet make any real noise on the ground.

"Who was he?" Maya asked, back in the foyer.

"That, Rose, was Freddy. He's one of the ones you'd best stay away from. See, most of us are just content to be here in a safe place, but there are always a few who just aren't domesticated. Aren't tamed. He's one of them."

"But . . . he looked nice."

"He's a wolf in sheep's clothing," Laila hissed, leading the way down the darkened hallway toward Mrs. Attleboro's office. "He's German."

"And?"

Laila rolled her eyes.

Maya wanted to protest. She didn't see how bad Freddy could, be but arguing with someone on her first day didn't seem like a good idea.

Back near Mrs. Attleboro's office was a staircase that Maya had previously failed to notice. The floating feeling, she noted as she climbed the steep steps, had been flickering and fading as her surroundings became more and more real, as the acknowledgement that this was her home had begun to sink in. That surreal feeling was completely shattered when Laila yanked open a door on the second floor, revealing a small room with six metal twin beds lined up on the walls, and proclaimed that this was where Maya would sleep.

Maya had to restrain herself from sinking to the floor, from willing herself, right there and then, to the grey beach.

"Are you okay?" Laila asked, frowning at Maya's tightened jaw.

"Yes." *No.*

Fight through it, one half of her said. *Suck it up. You've faced worse. No matter what they say, this is only temporary. You will find someone to trust. You will get out of here eventually.*

No, the other half sobbed. *This is the end. You're stuck here. No one will find you.* It snowballed, going on and on. *You lost your necklace. You'll never get home, never see Auntie or Scarlett again. How could you ever have thought you're the one in the prophecy?*

Maya sat down on one of the beds, feeling the springs beneath the thin mattress, no longer able to bear the voices screaming in her head. She tried to blink back tears—but they came anyway—and touched the spot on her chest where her necklace should be.

"Are you okay?" Laila asked again, sitting down beside Maya. The bed groaned under their combined weight.

Yes. No. Yes. No.

"No," Maya spat out.

"That's—that's fine. It's a hard transition."

Somewhere in the rational part of her brain, Maya could tell that Laila had had this conversation before.

"It's just . . . I don't know." With the hand that wasn't over her chest, Maya rubbed her eyes, trying to regain some composure. She sniffled. "Do you like it here?" The words fell out, hanging in midair, as she waited for Laila to either pick them up or let them crash to the ground.

"Do I like it here?" Laila rolled the words around in her hand. "No one really asks us that. I mean, Mrs. Attleboro's is the best place for us. We can move on from here. We can build lives." She sighed. "I've been here since I was about three, or so I'm told. I've never known my real birthday. Anyway, I've lived here for twelve years, I've grown up here, and I turned out okay. It's not a real home, but it's about as close as I was ever going to get. So, yes, I guess I do like it here. But what about you, Rose? You're attentive, you're interested, you're more than I ever was . . ." Laila stared at Maya, searching her face, finding her shocking green eyes.

"You want more than just a home . . . you want to be somebody. Who?"

"You're wrong," Maya answered quietly, looking directly at Laila. The flecks in her eyes swam perilously, and a feeling of emptiness seemed to consume her. "I don't want to be anyone. I'm . . . no one."

CHAPTER 4

Freddy

After a few silent minutes, Laila stood up. "I have to get you your uniform Stay here," she called to Maya. "I'll be right back."

Maya leaned against one of the walls. Cracked wallpaper poked at her back. She could hear faint footsteps on the third floor, and then Laila reemerged on the stairs, a dress, stockings, shoes, and a nightgown in her hands.

"We may need to tailor the dress a little," she said, inspecting the clothes, "but we'll see.

She held them out to Maya. "You can change here. Keep the nightgown under your bed."

Maya nodded as Laila retreated to the hallway. She nudged the door shut and made her way over to the bed by the window. Her bed. Sitting down, she took off her shoes and then began to undress, leaving her tunic on top of the bare mattress.

Maya pulled the dress, which was blue like Laila's, over her head. It slid on easily, and Maya looked down at herself.

She hardly recognized the body attached to her head. The dress, as unobtrusive, as plain as it was, still felt frilly and too nice, like a dress that you are forced to wear to a party. In the Land of the Clouds, Maya had avoided dresses as much as possible. She supposed that was why this one felt strange. Also, she realized, it was slightly too big and seemed to give the impression that she was undersized and short.

Next, she shoved the stockings on, biting her lip at their itchiness. Finally, she slid on her shoes, feeling her toes trying to squirm, to move around in the cramped space.

She held up a sleeve of the dress and brought to her nose. She recoiled almost immediately at the musty stench that radiated from the fabric and put her hands to her mouth, trying to breathe in the not-musty smell of her skin instead. In desperation, for that hadn't worked, she climbed onto her mattress and pressed her hands to the cold glass of the window, trying to find a way to open it. Unlocking it, she threw the sash up and let the morning air waft into the room.

Maya peered out the window. She could see Taleo Place down below looking as grimy as ever, and she could glimpse into the window across the way . . . the boys' building.

There was a knock on the door. "Rose, are you almost ready?"

Maya hurriedly pushed the sash down and relocked the window. She bent down, pulled a box out from under her bed, and stowed her tunic and nightgown there. Then she stood up, brushing dust off her dress. "All ready."

She rushed over to the door, her new shoes clacking on the floor, and wrenched it open.

Laila stared suspiciously at her. Maya's stomach flipped, hoping her cheeks weren't flushed from the fresh air. "Right," Laila said, looking distracted. "Let's get to class."

They trooped downstairs, and Maya followed Laila into the classroom. "Classes are grouped by age, so you'll be in this group here." Laila pointed to the first area. Then she swept forward, leaving Maya to catch up.

Laila stopped at the front of the room, just beside the teacher's desk. The teacher seemed young, in her twenties, and her dress was nicer than those of the children. "Yes?" she asked, her voice reedy.

"Miss Smith, this is Rose. She's going to be in your class."

Miss Smith smiled. It was a strange motion, stiff and wide. "How excellent."

Laila dipped her head and left the classroom.

Maya suddenly felt very alone, like a boat in the middle of the sea.

"Rose, would you please take a seat in the back? We have one open chair."

Maya nodded. "Yes, ma'am." She swallowed and, staring at her toes, made her way to a back table, trying to ignore the seven or eight pairs of eyes watching her.

She sat down. The seat was hard and wooden, like the table before her. Every set of eyes flicked back to Miss Smith, their owners' hands clasped neatly on their desks. Maya quickly adopted the same position, her back straight, her head high.

"Susie," Mrs. Smith instructed, "please bring a chalkboard back to Rose."

"Yes, ma'am," replied a sweet voice from the front of the room. Someone stood up, and at first all Maya could see was a honey-colored braid sweeping down a back. Then the person turned around, and Maya saw narrow, dark brown eyes and a small face.

Susie held out the chalkboard to Maya. Her hand was rough and calloused. She smiled and shot a dirty look at the person next to Maya, who—Maya turned—was . . . Freddy. The boy Laila had warned her about. Words of thanks died on Maya's tongue.

As Miss Smith resumed her lesson, Maya heard a snort coming from beside her. She turned to face her table partner.

His red hair was flaming, vibrant, lively. Messy and slightly curly, it burst with energy, but whether that energy was malicious was unclear. Freckles were carelessly sprayed across the face, as if a painter had made an accident and flicked his brush at the wrong moment. They made him seem reckless, daring. Beneath them, a small mouth twitched slightly in amusement. And his eyes were . . . Maya had always been sure that her eyes, with their shining specks of silver and gold, were the most magical eyes in the world. She saw now that she was wrong. These eyes weren't brown, weren't blue, weren't any color in the rainbow. Instead, they faded, constantly, imperceptibly, from a rich, powerful green the hue of forest leaves to a chocolate color that was creamy and sweet. Back and forth they went, back and forth, melting into each other. Maya could have watched them for an eternity, transfixed by their magical dance. Everything about this face seemed to flicker, seemed to change from one moment to the next, flipping from calm to reckless, entwined in a perfect choreography. And then the face spoke.

"I'm Freddy." The voice was quiet, inflected with a barely audible German accent.

Maya jerked her eyes away from Freddy and fixed them upon Miss Smith, staring at her, though her ears took in none of her lecture. Freddy didn't look evil, Maya thought. He didn't look normal either, but there was a spark that seemed to reside in him, powering him, and Maya felt that energy begin to soak into her skin.

"I'm Rose," she answered, still watching Miss Smith.

"I know."

That was arrogant, Maya thought. "*I know.*" Part of her bristled, and yet part of her wanted to hear more. The bristle won: Maya responded with stiff silence.

Freddy didn't speak to her again for the rest of the morning, and Maya didn't try to talk to him, but something inside her had stirred. It watched him. He seemed to possess a sort of familiarity, a sort of comfort that Maya lacked.

As the grandfather clock tolled the hours away, Maya

remained only half focused on the lesson. Not only did she know how to write and read in English, unlike some of her classmates, but she could do so better than any of them. History and current events were of no interest to her, try as she might to enjoy studying them, for she already knew of much more interesting events that would take place in the near future—namely, the First World War.

Finally, the grandfather clock rang to announce noon. This seemed to be the lunch break, for the class began to pass their chalkboards up to the front of the room and stood. Freddy was the only boy in the class, Maya noted.

The class shuffled out of the room toward the scent of food that was drifting out of the open dining room door. Maya, at the back of the class line, was bouncing slightly, impatient, her stomach rumbling. She had not eaten since— since the train ride to 15 Harding Street, she realized with a shock.

She was still in the front hall when someone tugged at her sleeve. Freddy was standing on the front stoop, his arm outstretched. His eyes swirled mesmerizingly. "Come out here," he hissed.

Maya bit her lip. *Lunch. Freddy. Lunch. Freddy.* Freddy, she decided, was far more intriguing than lunch.

She stepped outside. Freddy pulled the door shut behind her. The two of them stood on the front steps. Maya looked up at the sky. The clouds had vanished during the morning, and a streak of sunlight shot down upon 50 Taleo Place. Maya sighed contentedly. Spring air always smelled the best, especially in the sun.

Freddy tugged on her sleeve again.

"Who are you?" he asked, his voice intent.

"What do you mean 'who am I'? I'm Rose." The lie was becoming easier to say every time.

Freddy rolled his eyes. "I know that." There he went

again with his *I knows*. "But *who are you?*"

"No one." Again, the words felt like a sucker punch to Maya's stomach.

"No one . . ." Freddy mused. He hopped down the stairs and onto the street. Maya followed him. He was the same size, the same build as she was, she realized. "I don't think you're no one."

"I am. What do you mean?"

"You don't hate me." The lightness of his voice had vanished. He sounded inquisitive, wondering, not as cocky as before.

"Why would I hate you?"

"They all hate me. Everyone here." Freddy kicked at the ground. "But you don't."

"Again, why would I hate you?" Maya was confused.

"Because."

"Because you're German?"

Freddy looked up at her, his swirling eyes meeting her speckled ones. "Yes."

Maya snorted. "Well, that's a stupid reason."

"But to them it's a reason. Even though I've been here since I was four, they still hate me."

"Like I said, that's stupid." The conversation seemed to be going in circles.

"I'm going to be in the army when I grow up. When I'm old enough, I'll join. Maybe even before then if I can lie about my birthday. Then they won't question me." There was a hunger in his voice, a daringness and a sense purpose that resonated with Maya. She used to have that feeling, she knew. But the time when she could time travel, when she was carefree, traveling the Earth, believing she was the one in the prophecy, already seemed to be a long, long time ago.

"Well," she said to him, determined not to betray her feelings, "that's a very good goal, I guess."

"Yeah," he said. "But anyway, I just wanted to tell you this: You're a good person, Rose. I want to be like you."

"You don't even know me." The words tasted like poison to Maya. Freddy *didn't* know her, didn't know that she was nothing. Or, at least, he didn't believe it.

"But still . . ." he pushed on. "Will you be friends with me?"

Maya looked at him, at the crazy hair, at the impetuous freckles, at the eyes that shifted magically, that held a hunger that Maya found familiar, that were bold and exciting.

"Sure. Friends," she said slowly, savoring the words.

They shook on it, and then Freddy went back to the boys' building and Maya retreated up the steps of 50 Taleo Place for lunch.

CHAPTER 5

The Trip

Over the next few days, Maya became more and more aware of a fire stirring in her stomach. It had been stamped out, she realized, but its embers were being stoked once more. Every time she saw Freddy, she felt two things. First, a wave of relief that washed over her, dowsing the tension that clenched her shoulder blades together. Then, a warm feeling, a feeling like she was at home. Somehow, inexplicably, Freddy reminded her of home, of her friends back in the Land of the Clouds.

Every morning they sat next to each other in class, sharing notes they scribbled on the edges of their chalkboards. Sometimes, in their notes, they made fun of the kids in their class or what the teacher was saying. For Maya, this was great fun, as she never learned anything from Miss Smith anyway. Freddy seemed to be the same way. And, she noted, when he smiled, his teeth were white and shiny, just like hers.

In the afternoons, Maya had to do chores with the other girls in her room. They washed dishes, swept floors, and cleaned windows. Maya was silent the whole time, not wanting to talk to her companions. Besides, she told herself, it wasn't as though they were trying to include her. They usually asked her a few questions to get her to join in, but none of them seemed to care to continue the conversation from there. Instead, they resorted to murmuring various inside jokes to each other and laughing quietly.

The best time of day, however, was the hour before supper. That was when the inhabitants of Mrs. Attleboro's

Orphanage for Abandoned Children went outside and played on the grimy street, trying their best not to dirty their clothes. It was the one time of day when the boys and girls were all together.

Maya always stayed by the front stoop waiting, feeling awkward, until Freddy came bounding out of the boys' building. Her heart ached as she saw the hateful glares others threw at him. She couldn't imagine being subjected to such a thing.

Once Freddy joined Maya, they would race around the other children, darting past older boys and girls who looked nervously at each other, past little kids drawing with rocks on the street, laughing. So long as they ran and played, nothing else seemed to matter.

It was during this hour, once they were tired out and sat, panting, on the steps, that Maya learned more about Freddy. He talked about his past a lot, she thought, especially for someone whose past made people dislike him. And he was constantly talking about his future. He rambled on about different branches of the military, about battle formations and weapons. His mystical eyes would grow even stronger then, as he seemed to will his future into being.

It was in those moments, when Maya saw the wall of determination behind Freddy's eyes, that she wanted to tell him about Auntie and the Land, her parents and the necklace, the prophecy and her power to time travel, about all the special things that had been forced down inside her. But she couldn't. And so she shut herself off, and though Freddy knocked fiercely on her door, she didn't let him in.

There was no point in him knowing, Maya reassured herself. She had been wrong about everything. He surely wouldn't want to know about her failures and mistakes. She let him talk away, and though she asked him questions, although she remarked things about her day, she never said what was really on her mind.

And yet every night, as she lay in bed staring through a crack in the curtains watching the night sky, she wished she had told him, for she could feel herself slipping. There was only so much longer she felt she could stay here, confined to the dead end of Taleo Place. If she only could tell Freddy about her past, then maybe the two of them could find a way to contact the Land of the Clouds. But she never did. And every night she would turn away from the window and press her face into her thin pillow and let the tears fall, let them seep into the cotton where no one could find them.

It was Friday morning. Fractured bits of sunlight speared the windows of the dining room, landing on the tables. Maya pushed her spoon idly around her porridge. The rest of her table was talking quietly. She wondered if they'd heard her crying the night before.

The sharp sound of footsteps resounded in the hall, and Mrs. Attleboro appeared in the dining room doorway. The hum of voices stopped. Mrs. Attleboro coughed to get everyone's attention, though that was unnecessary, seeing as they were all already watching her. "I have an announcement." Her voice was clear and concise, out of place among the specks of dust flying through the air.

Maya hid a smirk at her words. That was also unnecessary. There was no reason she would be there unless she had an announcement. If Freddy had been sitting next to Maya, instead of Georgia-what's-her-name, they might have shared a quiet laugh, but alas . . .

"This weekend," Mrs. Attleboro continued, still standing directly in the doorway, "there shall be a trip to the seaside. I'll be taking all children aged eight to twelve."

The noise in the dining room went up again, as people murmured about how lucky the eight-to-twelve-year-olds were and how unlucky the rest of them were.

Mrs. Attleboro coughed again. Silence reigned once more. "This trip will be tomorrow, Saturday. We will leave early in the morning and come back in the evening. There should be eighteen people on the trip, including the boys. I know who is coming, so please don't try to sneak on. I would hate to have to give out extra chores."

With that, Mrs. Attleboro turned on her heel and marched out of the room. A rumble rose up in the dining room like a volcano before it erupts.

Maya had nothing to say to anyone at her table. *Freddy*, she was thinking. She wanted to talk to Freddy. And so she sat silently as bits of conversations drifted by her ear.

"D'you think I could pass for twelve if I bribed Joanna to let me have her spot?"

"It's so unfair! They always get to go on trips."

"I can't wait! I'm so excited!"

"She said the boys are coming too, right?

Finally, breakfast was over. Maya rushed over to her classroom. The tables were empty, the eight chairs neatly pushed in. Not even Miss Smith was there yet. Maya made her way to the back of the class, pulled out her chair, and, tucking her dress beneath her, sat down.

She listened as people made their way toward the classroom, their voices growing louder and louder. Then they emerged, some of them splitting off to go to different classes, some of them heading into Miss Smith's class where she was sitting.

"Morning, Rose," said someone in front of her, their voice sweet and honeyed. Maya looked around. Susie was standing a little ways away, smiling, though it was as though her face was made of plastic, barely able to bend. Her eyes were beady and dark.

"Morning," Maya responded hesitantly. She could never decide whether Susie was nice or not.

She was spared any further conversation, however, by the arrival of Freddy. He brushed past all of the girls making their way into their seats—much to their dislike; there were many glares fired at him—and plopped down beside Maya.

"Morning." He sounded out of breath.

"Morning." Maya stared at him suspiciously.

"Did you—" they both began. "No, you first."

"The trip," Maya said, taking advantage of the fact that Freddy was catching his breath.

"Yeah, the trip." Freddy smiled. "It's going to be fun, I think. I ran over here to tell you."

"You ran?"

He nodded.

"Is that why you're panting?"

He nodded again, his hair bouncing slightly.

Maya shook her head. *Boys*, she thought. She had been waiting to tell Freddy about the trip, but she wouldn't have *run* to do it. Well, she considered, she might've.

Miss Smith appeared, however, before they could continue talking. And, since they weren't using the chalkboards that day, they could pass no notes. Still, Maya could sense the exuberance inside Freddy, an exuberance she shared.

The day passed in a rather boring fashion after the announcement at breakfast. Though everyone was still excited about the trip, the initial shock had worn off, and it was only a small topic of conversation through lunch and afternoon chores.

Outside in the evening, before supper, the older and younger kids watched the eight-to-twelve-year-olds with jealousy, for they carried themselves with a self-important air, chins up, strutting around the dead-end alley like pigeons in a city square.

Later, when Maya and the other girls in her room readied themselves for bed, punching their pillows into more comfortable shapes—if the pillows moved at all—Mrs. Attleboro appeared in the doorway.

She knocked on the door to get the girls' attention. "I hope you all sleep well. Those of you who are between ages eight and twelve, please be up early. I will stop by every room in the morning, but I do not wish to have to rouse anyone."

"Yes, ma'am," Maya and one other girl, Alice, said. She was ten, Maya thought, or somewhere around there. At any rate, they were the only two in the room who were going on the trip. The rest were too old, and one was too young.

One of the older girls turned out the gaslight, and darkness filled the room. Maya lay awake, as she always did, watching through the curtains. The moon was full tonight, and it felt like a guardian angel high in the sky, watching the whole city with its pockmarked face.

A pain shot through Maya, dull but pronounced. Just briefly, she remembered the way the moon looked in the Land of the Clouds, how it was always so clear and bright, and how, when it was full, it seemed to take up the entire sky. With these thoughts in her head, she fell into a deep but restless sleep.

It was hardly dawn when Maya awoke. Someone was shaking her shoulder. "Get off," Maya murmured sleepily.

"Get up," a voice countered.

Maya sat up slowly, her eyes still hazy with sleep. She rubbed them and blinked, looking around into the darkened room. Alice stood at the side of Maya's bed. "Get up," she repeated, her voice soft. "Mrs. Attleboro'll be coming by in only a few minutes."

"Fine, fine." Maya rose and stretched, then pulled her dress, stockings, and shoes on. "Okay. Let's go."

They crept through the dark, out into the hallway and downstairs to the dining room. A few girls were already gathered. They sat at their tables, rubbing their eyes and whispering excitedly.

There was an invisible buzz in the air, the sound of eager preparation, the feeling that comes before an adventure. Maya let it whoosh through her skin, let it set her nerves tingling, let her despondency fall away for just a moment. After all, she was going on a trip. She was going to see the ocean.

"I can't wait," Alice said. Maya could see her eyes light up from within. "I haven't been out of here in so long."

Maya smiled. "Yeah, me too."

A few minutes passed, and the last stragglers came down the stairs, entering the dining room. Then Mrs. Attleboro appeared.

"All right," she said, still as stiff as a plank of wood. "Let's go."

She led the way out of 50 Taleo Place. The boys met them on the street, and together they began to troop down the lane.

Maya and Freddy walked together and shivered, looking up at the inky black windows they passed, which seemed to be devoid of all soul and life. They were eerie— more than eerie.

As the group got closer to the boulevard, Maya noticed the streetlamps. Oddly, there were no streetlamps at the end of Taleo Place; here, however, the orange light flooded parts of the cracked street.

They marched down the empty main boulevard, feeling the early morning silence all around them. There was hardly anyone out as they passed street after street, slowly wending their way toward the heart of the city.

They reached the train station soon after the sun came up. All around her, Maya heard "Wow" and "Amazing." She tried to join in, but the smile on her face was false. She couldn't be amazed by this station, not when she'd been here over a hundred years in the future.

As they boarded the train, Maya sat down, feeling numb again, as though the train she was on had just run her over. It wasn't so long ago, she realized, she had boarded a train traveling out of London.

When the train began to move, Maya couldn't gasp at its lurches like Freddy, nor share in the joy behind his eyes. Instead, she felt herself reliving her failure all over again. She could almost feel the aches and pains she had felt on the last train she had taken. She sat next to Freddy, watching his eager expression, so young and carefree, and touched her chest, wishing she could disappear to the grey beach, wishing she could have her necklace back.

The sense of loss was so strong that Maya excused herself from her seat. She stumbled to a mostly empty car and sat down in a corner. She needed to try one more time. She needed to know. And so, with dread pricking her spine like icicles, she took a deep breath and concentrated. She imagined going down to the grey beach, imagined swimming through the Tunnel of Time. Finally she saw it. It was hazy, faint, distant. But it was there. The grey beach. She stepped forward, trying to see through the film that obstructed her vision. She took another step. All was quiet. There was hardly any wind, and the waves barely made a sound. Strange. Another step . . .

Her eyes flew open, and, panting, she looked around. She was in the train car. Sweat streamed down her back. And then tears streamed down her face.

———————————————

It was a while before Maya could rejoin the others. But none of them, not even Freddy, seemed to have noticed her absence, for they were too busy gawking at the beautiful countryside, at the precious emerald fields, at the sparkling blue sky dotted with clouds. Maya stared too, but only for something outside herself to focus on.

Soon the train began to slow, hissing and screeching as it rolled to a stop. The children pressed their grubby hands against the windows, much to the chagrin of Mrs. Attleboro, who scolded them for tarnishing the clean glass.

They all scampered outside as soon as the train doors opened, shouting, relishing the fresh late-morning sunlight on their faces.

"It's so warm!" Freddy exclaimed, his grin wide.

Maya had to agree. The heat wasn't oppressive, however, but welcoming, cocooning. It felt like a soft fireside.

Mrs. Attleboro shepherded the children out of the small station. Maya caught a glimpse of the name of the town of which they were in. "Southend-on-Sea," a small sign said. Not Shellside. Maya breathed a sigh of relief that she didn't know she had been holding in.

They skipped through the cobblestone streets—well, the children skipped, their laughs light and clear—and Mrs. Attleboro speed-walked along in front of them, as rigid as ever.

Soon they reached the limits of the town and were making their way up a few low hills that overlooked the sea. The children were sweating by the time they could feel the sea wind brush against their face, but it was worth it. The ocean sparkled, nearly calm except for a few tall waves that roared and crashed onto the rocks at the foot of the hills.

"Children," Mrs. Attleboro called. "We shall stay here

on this hill. You may wander, but do not go out of sight. I have food in this basket"—she held up a large picnic basket—"and we shall eat lunch in one hour. Now, go be free!"

The children ran and yelled, crossing back and forth on the hilltop over the soft, dewy grasses. The air pulsed with joy and happiness as all delighted in this respite from London's grey buildings.

Maya and Freddy sat on the edge of the hill, staring out at the sea.

"I've never seen the sea before." Freddy seemed to be in awe.

Maya longed to say "I have." She longed to tell him everything, but she instead sucked in her chest. "Neither have I."

The sea didn't keep Freddy speechless for long. He began to talk about his past, about his parents, about how when he was older, he would sail the sea and feel the wind rush through his hair all day long.

Freddy rambled on, the near-noon light hitting him full in the face. He talked more than he ever had before. The sea breeze seemed to refresh him, and there was more light behind his swirling eyes than Maya had ever seen.

I won't let him in. I won't. I won't, she told herself, chanting it over and over. The words were on the tip of her tongue. *Hold them back. Hold them back.*

"I'm going to go to sea someday, Rose," Freddy said, staring longingly at the gorgeous blue waves that rolled and crashed, unbeatable, in the ocean.

"Don't call me that." The words slipped out, a venomous snake, before Maya could stop them. *Come back,* she thought. *Come back.*

"Why?" Freddy looked confused.

Don't say anything. Don't—"It's not my name." Another snake pushing its way out. "My name is Maya."

"But why—?"

In the end, she told him everything. She told him about the Land of the Clouds—and her heart almost split open as she recalled Auntie and Scarlett and even Sir Galiston. She talked about the prophecy, about her parents, about her necklace. She explained how she had jumped to Earth. She told him about the grey beach and how it had grown more and more hostile until it would no longer let her in. Now tears swam down her cheeks, racing each other, dripping down onto the soft green grass beneath. She talked about 15 Harding Street and the bicyclist, about how she'd lost her necklace, her ability to time travel. She told him that she had been wrong, foolish, stupid.

Finally, she buried her face in her hands and remained that way for several minutes, drowning in her loss, tense, anticipating the moment Freddy would decide she wasn't good enough to be his friend. The moment he would walk away.

Finally, she looked up. And there he was, still sitting next to her. He looked lost in thought. The specks of silver and gold glittered in Maya's eyes. "I'm sorry," she muttered.

"No." Freddy sounded as if he was in a dream. He sounded like he was floating, seeing a world that Maya couldn't. "Don't be sorry." He sounded more grounded now and turned to look Maya in the eye. "I believe you."

Maya froze. She could barely breathe. "You what?"

"I believe you." Now Freddy was ramping up, getting louder, gaining momentum. "I always knew there was something else in this world. I always knew there was more than I could know." He was grinning. "There is more. It all makes sense."

"I guess . . ." Maya hadn't expected this reaction.

If it was possible, Freddy would've been shooting off sparks. He brimmed. He overflowed with excitement, and this time Maya laughed—really laughed—for what felt like the first time in years. She was aware of the happiness around her, aware of the way the air tasted like cotton candy. Someone believed her. Someone understood what she was going through.

"It makes sense, it makes sense!" Freddy said. "And I think you were right. I think you are the one in the prophecy."

"But I'm not. I know I'm not." Maya said incredulously.

"No, I'm sure you are. It fits. Everything you said about your parents, about the voices in your dreams, about the laugh you heard on the hill by the lake. They all point to you being the one in the prophecy."

Maya felt a jolt go through her, and she quivered. She was alive, really alive. The pieces were coming together now, just as they had way back when in the Land of the Clouds. *I am the one. I am the one.*

"You are the one," Freddy said, seeming to read her mind.

"*I am the one,*" she repeated. "And I'll defeat the OCT. I will. I'll . . . run away from Mrs. Attleboro's and I'll find them. I'll go back to 15 Harding Street and . . ."

Maya was picking her burden back up, the burden she had left in an alleyway in London on the night she'd arrived. It was heavy, sure, but it was comfortable, familiar. She didn't stagger under its weight like she had the last time she'd carried it. No. She was upright. She was taking her destiny into her own hands again.

Maya breathed. The air had never tasted so good.

"And I can come too?" Freddy asked.

"Yes! Yes, you must. I wouldn't have figured it all out if it wasn't for you."

"Oh, yes! Thank you, thank you!" Freddy was about to burst with joy. He swelled up, and his face broke out in the biggest grin.

And then they heard a voice. "Lunchtime!" Mrs. Attleboro called.

"But first," Maya said. "Lunch."

Scarlett sat on the cold, rocky ground. Maya's necklace dangled from her fingers, glinting in the light of the campfire she was beside. "Auntie?" she called softly.

It was a couple of weeks since they had been to 15 Harding Street, and something had shifted between the two of them. They were no longer two people bound together, struggling to free themselves from one another, but instead now of one mind. They embraced their struggle. It made them stronger.

Auntie looked up from where she was perched on a small rock next to the fire. The two of them were in a cave, the walls of which were lined with small cracks and crevices that pierced the slate-grey stone. The fire cast strange shadows along the walls. "Yes?" Her eyes were weary, too calm considering the storm that they were in.

"I think I'm ready." Scarlett held up the necklace. In contrast, her eyes were sharp and focused, her breath determined.

Technically, they had been ready to find Maya since the moment they had found the necklace. An object with such a strong connection to its owner was sure to show them her location. And yet, when Scarlett had tried, she had failed. Whether it was from her own sorrow and inability, or some other force, she didn't know. But now ... now felt right.

Scarlett clenched the necklace and shut her eyes, concentrating on viewing Maya, on whatever secrets the necklace held in store. She was walking through space, through emptiness. Then came the past. Memories whirled past Scarlett as she forced her way through them. Now was not the time to explore history; now was the time to see the present, the future. Finally, the memories ended. Scarlett immersed herself in the sounds and smells of the new scene.

There was a 20th-century train. It tooted its horn and shuffled along the tracks, clicking as it went. But something told Scarlett that was not what she was looking for. She walked into the train and passed through it as though it were nothing more than mist. *The future. The future.* Scarlett blinked.

And then she was standing in front of a building, a grimy townhouse at the end of a dead-end street. Its windows were clean, harshly reflecting the sunlight above. "Mrs. Attleboro's Orphanage for Abandoned Children, 50 Taleo Place," a sign read. Scarlett felt her heart lurch with excitement. That was the place. She was sure of it. That was where they would find Maya. She prepared to exit the scene, to reenter the cave, the real world, when it caught her eye—a flame bursting through one of those shiny windows. Scarlett could feel its heat on her face. And then another, and another. Smoke poured out of the building.

Scarlett's face became pale and sweaty as she watched. *No, no, no.*

Her eyes wrenched open in the cave. Auntie looked concernedly into their hazel irises. "What did you see?"

"I found her." Scarlett was breathless. "Mrs. Attleboro's Orphanage for Abandoned Children, 50 Taleo Place, London, 1910," she rattled off. "But something bad is going to happen. We have to hurry."

Auntie didn't need telling twice. She put out their campfire, collected their bags, and then held out her hand for Scarlett to grab. Together, they vanished into the faded meadow.

―――――――――――

After lunch, which consisted of all of the children sitting down on the ground munching happily on their sandwiches and swatting away bugs, Maya and Freddy retreated back to the hillside overlooking the sea. In the background, they could hear gleeful laughs as some of the children took to smashing anthills around their picnic area.

Maya was shivering, though she wasn't cold or nervous. There was simply a buzz running through her body that threatened to light her up, to electrify her. Over and over again she asked Freddy, "You really believe me?"

Then he would smile, and match the slightly crazed look in her eyes, and respond, "Yes, Maya. I do."

They sat in silence for a few minutes and watched puffy clouds hop by overhead. Finally, Maya asked, though she felt it was more to the world in general than to Freddy directly, "What do we do now?"

Freddy shrugged, but not in an apathetic way. Rather, more cluelessly. "Repeat the prophecy again?"

Maya took a deep breath and began to recite:

> *"The child born on the first of two*
> *Who knows it is their fate*
> *Shall harness powers most impressive*
> *To defeat the enemies of eight."*

The words felt hallowed, too sacred for this little hill on Earth.

"Right. So we know what it means." Freddy rubbed his hands together, his eyes narrowed, determined. Maya let his focus soak into her.

"Yeah. As far as prophecies go, it's pretty clear. I was born on the first of two, and I know, or I knew, it was my fate." Maya felt herself fall slightly off of the pedestal that Freddy had raised her up on.

"It is your fate," Freddy interjected, his eyes in their perpetual fade. "It is."

Maya took another breath. "It is. It is." She climbed back up.

"The next part doesn't apply to me, though," she said. "'Harness powers most impressive'? I haven't got any powers yet." She frowned and gritted her teeth.

"But it says you *shall*. Maybe not yet." Freddy sounded like he was trying to salvage his own dreams as much as Maya's. "You'll get powers. I'm sure of it."

But the line had driven something into Maya's heart, and it wedged there uncomfortably. *You don't have powers. You will never have powers.* Maya swallowed and returned her focus to Freddy.

"The last line," he said. "What is it again?"

"'To defeat the enemies of eight.'"

"That makes perfect sense. You'll defeat the OCT. And I'll help you do it." Hunger glinted in his eyes, across his freckles, in his perfect white teeth.

"Yes. Yes." Maya immersed herself in Freddy's positivity. When she reemerged, she was so full of it, she was dripping it. "I am the one. I am. I am. It fits in. It fits." Her eyes shone in the sunlight as it bounced across the waves. Maya could remember how she felt up in the Land of the Clouds on that afternoon when she first truly realized what the prophecy said. That same feeling, one of puzzle pieces clicking into place, now filled her entire being. Subconsciously, Maya brought her hand to her chest. But of course the necklace wasn't there. Only a shadow of it, a phantom pain.

They sat in silence for a few minutes more, watching the waves crash upon the beach. Maya knew she would never tire of watching it. Its power was so raw, so natural, so earthly. Her grey beach—if she could ever visit it again— could never match that.

Maya's thoughts jumped around. And then—"15

Harding Street."

Freddy, who had been knotting a piece of grass, looked up, his hair bobbing up and down. "What?"

"We'll run."

Freddy sighed. "What?" he repeated.

It was only then that Maya acknowledged his presence. "Let's go to 15 Harding Street. You know, the place on my necklace. The place I was trying to reach last time?"

"Okay . . ."

"I barely made it there last time, but I'm sure I can now. I know about Earth. I don't need to travel around. We can just go straight to Harding Street."

"So . . . when will we go?"

"Early tomorrow morning. When everyone is in bed. They'll start the search in London, and by then we'll be long gone."

Freddy grinned. "I can't wait."

Maya returned his smile, a hunger she hadn't felt in a long time filling her eyes. "We're going to save the world."

CHAPTER 6

The Attack

Maya awoke in the pitch-black darkness. She lay still for a moment and listened to the heavy breathing of her roommates. And then excitement coursed through her. She and Freddy were leaving. Now. They were leaving now.

Careful not to let her mattress squeak, she stood up and dressed in her old tunic. The fabric was soft and comforting.

The door to her room was oddly silent as she pushed it open. As were the stairs. It seemed as though everything was holding its breath in the dark. As she crept downstairs, the grandfather clock sounded, muffled behind the study doors. It rang once, twice, three times, four times.

And then, from her position in the front hall in the eerie quiet that followed, she heard heavy footsteps coming down the street.

Auntie and Scarlett were teleporting as fast as they could. Passed between them was a certain sense of déjà vu. The last time they had been rushing to meet Maya ...

No. They would not allow it to happen again.

Soon the lights of London were visible. Big Ben tolled four times as they were sucked into the city.

They were so close ...

Maya's heart pounded. That couldn't be Freddy; his footsteps didn't sound like that. So who was it? With a bad feeling in her chest, she unlocked the door and pushed it open a crack, just enough so that she could peer out into Taleo Place.

Her pulse climbed in her throat as she looked out in the dark. She could just barely make out the silhouette of a figure marching toward the dead end, toward her. She blinked, for it seemed like there was more than one figure. There were two, three, four . . . eight in total.

She stuck her head back inside and closed the door, leaning against it, breathing hard. Her eyes darted frantically, looking for anything, anything to stop them. Because she was sure that they would need stopping, and that she was going to be the one stopping them. Just her.

She thought and thought, all the while hearing the footsteps grow louder and louder. There was nothing she could think of, not on the first floor anyway. *The kitchen.* She ran downstairs as fast as she could. She no longer cared if she woke people up as she thundered to the kitchen, grabbed the first thing she saw, which was a pan, and raced back up to the front door.

The footsteps were nearly on the stoop now, coming closer, closer, as she tried to keep her breath steady, forcing the memory of her parents, of the lake, of the people in the city who had seemed to be after her, into the background. It didn't matter how they had caught up to her. They would pay for it.

As she stood, tense, battle-ready, the other inhabitants of 50 Taleo Place seemed to have been roused. Doors opened and shut, and worried voices echoed around in the early morning stillness.

Maya saw the flickering figure of Mrs. Attleboro emerge from her office and begin to climb the stairs, already threatening to punish people for not being in bed. And then there was a knock on the door. Maya swayed slightly, her vision becoming fuzzy around the edges. They were here. They were going to take her away, just because she was the one in the prophecy. And there was no one to help her. No one would understand why she needed protecting. They didn't even know that her name was Maya. Well, no one but Freddy. But Freddy was across the street. Which, at the moment, felt like an ocean away.

There was another knock. The commotion upstairs came to a halt. Silence. A third knock. Maya didn't move.

There was a muffled voice coming from upstairs. Maya didn't hear the words, but she recognized its stiff sharpness. A bunch of other people seemed to reply in assent, and then there were footsteps on the stairs. Mrs. Attleboro was coming down.

Maya felt frozen, a deer caught in headlights. To stay where she was would mean that Mrs. Attleboro would find her. To move would mean that she risked Mrs. Attleboro being exposed to the wrath of the figures outside the door.

Mrs. Attleboro had finished walking down the stairs. She was moving along the hallway, and Maya could tell that she was near the place where the gas lamp on the ceiling was. One more step and she would light it. One more step and she would see Maya.

Maya wasn't conscious of the decision she made. Her feet suddenly shifted as though they had a mind of their own. They dragged her into the dining room and stopped. Mrs. Attleboro turned on the light and, oblivious to the danger waiting directly beyond the front door, strode toward it.

There was a click—to Maya as loud as a gunshot— as Mrs. Attleboro unlocked the door, and then a horrible sticky noise as she wrenched it open.

Safely hidden in the shadows, though unable to see beyond the front door, Maya watched as Mrs. Attleboro's taut expression morphed into nervous surprise and then tautened again. "Hello," she said, her voice a rope that had been pulled tight. "How may I help you? And what, might I ask, brings you here at this hour?"

Maya couldn't make out the response; all she could hear was an icy hissing, the sound of fingers creeping up your spine.

"I am afraid that is private information. You shall have to file a request." Mrs. Attleboro's voice trembled ever so slightly.

A black-gloved hand rose and, in an instant, withdrew a dagger from its belt. The point, only half a foot away, was aimed at Mrs. Attleboro, whose face contorted into pure horror.

The hissing voice repeated what it had said before. Maya crept as close to the door of the dining room as she could, pan in hand.

"No, we do not. There is no Maya here," Mrs. Attleboro responded. The wire had bent, and her voice was shaky.

Maya froze once again. They were looking for her. She had to get out of the building.

Meanwhile, the dagger twirled around in the gloved hand.

"I swear. I swear!" Mrs. Attleboro's voice grew more high pitched. "There's no Maya here."

Another hiss as Maya's eyes rested on the front window . . . she could open it and jump out. She moved, careful to make no sound greater than the monstrous beating of her heart.

"Y-yes," Mrs. Attleboro answered to the next question. "Come in. The children are upstairs. But—" her gaze flicked to the dagger—"please promise not to hurt them."

The window was open. As the cloaked figures entered 50 Taleo Place, evidently to search it until they found Maya, Maya herself, pan still in hand, slipped through the open window and landed on the cold street.

Maya knew she should run for it. She knew that she should forget about the enemies now trooping through the orphanage, drop the pan, and sprint out of the city as fast as she could. That was what a logical person would do. But she wasn't feeling logical. She wanted to fight them, and she wanted to win. The urge nearly caused a tic in her eye, it was so strong.

As she stood in the corner of the street, lights came on in 50 Taleo Place. She glimpsed figures moving in the rooms, in her room. *No. No, no, no.* Maya bowed her head, her cheeks flushed with shame as she mentally berated herself. When they searched her room, they would find that she was missing. That Rose was missing. It wouldn't take them long to put two and two together.

The knowledge that she should run was even stronger now. And her feet wanted to, but her brain forced them to remain rooted to the spot. She wasn't running away.

Maya heard the roar of outrage as the cloaked figures realized she was gone. It rebounded through the street, through the whole city, it seemed.

Lights burst on in the boys' building across the street. Now they were up too.

And then the door to 50 Taleo Place opened. Maya squirmed as people came flooding out, all of them still in their nightgowns. The girls of 50 Taleo Place lined up in the street, muttering as small pebbles pricked their bare feet. Some younger ones cried softly, hushed by older ones.

Last came Mrs. Attleboro and six cloaked figures. Maya frowned. Where had the other two gone? Then she saw figures still moving in the building.

One of the black figures pointed at the boys' building. Maya didn't see it ask anything since its face was in shadow, but Mrs. Attleboro's mouth moved quaveringly in response.

Two figures marched across the street and knocked

on the door.

Just then, from a third-floor window, a face peered out. A wide face with red hair. Maya looked sharply up at Freddy. His eyes wandered over the crowd of people, and then he saw her. He was staring straight at her. She jerked her head slightly. *Don't tell.* He nodded almost imperceptibly and then disappeared.

Within another few minutes there was a yell, and the boys of the orphanage were filing onto the street. Maya tried to back further into the dead end, but there was nowhere for her to go.

A line of boys stood a few feet away. She slinked back, trying to make herself smaller, but then—

"Hey." It wasn't spoken loudly, but it reverberated in Maya's ears. Her breath caught in her throat and her heart seemed to stop for a moment. "What are you doing?" the boy who'd seen her asked. The kids around him turned to see what he was looking at, their eyes piercing Maya like a thousand daggers.

"Mrs. Attleboro," the boy called, his sandy hair standing out in the dark. He raised his hand. "I found a kid not in line."

Maya forced herself to remain calm as an excited murmur rose from the black-cloaked figures. And then there was no more calm. Her cover had been blown. There was no better time to attack, Maya decided. And with that, she rammed through the hoard of children, directly at her enemies.

Her pan was held in front of her like a sword, ready to swing at her opponents. When the four figures saw her coming, their cloaks whirled around like winds in a storm, and they drew their daggers.

"So, child, we meet at last," one said softly, sounding like a sizzle on a frying pan. It took Maya a moment to realize they were speaking Cloudian.

"I'm no child," she snarled back. "I'm the one." And then she launched herself at them—banging one's arm with the pan, causing him to drop his dagger.

Maya picked it up, feeling charged with electricity. She and the figures circled each other, and then they all simultaneously attacked her. Maya's fighting instincts took over. She parried with her pan, wielding it like a club, and her dagger slipped in and out like a snake, hunting for an opening to strike.

She poured her focus into the battle, completely oblivious to the gapes of the children. Out of the corner of her eye, she noticed Freddy pushing his way through the crowd. He appeared by her side, and they began to work as a team, Maya keeping the figures distracted as she assailed them with her pan and dagger, Freddy throwing punches and kicks, trying to trip and bruise them. They worked fluidly, as if they had always done this, weaving around their opponents, spinning webs for them to fall in. Energy flowed between them, each feeding off the other. They were consumed with the fight. And so it was a large surprise when a voice, a familiar voice that was as rich as honey, called, "Maya!"

Maya whirled around, turning her back on the battle for a moment. Auntie and Scarlett were sprinting toward her, daggers in their hands. Maya paused for another second as her heart filled with joy, and her cheeks flushed. Auntie and Scarlett joined in, and together the four of them drove the four figures back. But it couldn't last forever. The figures were rebounding, coming back stronger. The four who had gone to search the orphanage buildings had returned. Maya prepared to rally all of her strength into one final attack, and then someone snagged her sleeve, and someone else caught Freddy. She caught one last look at her enemies, with an octagon emblazoned on their back of their robes, and then she was submerged in darkness.

CHAPTER 7

Reunited

Maya was standing in a small dell filled with long grasses and completely devoid of any human life. Freddy stood on one side of her, and Auntie and Scarlett on the other.

"Who are you?" Freddy asked, one eyebrow creeping up.

No one answered Freddy's question. Maya looked into Auntie and Scarlett's faces, stared at the hazel eyes, at the blue, watery eyes. They seemed to be doing the same thing, drinking in Maya's appearance, soaking it up. Tears burst forth in both of their eyes, and they ran to hug her, wrapping her in a warm embrace, something Maya had not felt in a long, long time.

Auntie buried her head in Maya's shoulder and didn't let go, while Maya just stared into the distance as emotions bubbled within her—relief and love and something else too, something not as pleasant . . .

Scarlett, who had pulled out of the hug, leaving Auntie and Maya alone, couldn't stop grinning through her tears. She shook her head again and again, disbelieving. Yet even so, Maya noticed her gaze flicking suspiciously to Freddy, her mouth slipping into a small frown.

After a while, though, Maya wanted to pull away from the hug as well. She was sore from standing too long, and she felt an animosity growing like a tumor in the back of her brain. It was all fine and well that Auntie and Scarlett had found her, but she didn't need them. She had been doing just fine on her own. She and Freddy had had a plan, and they had come so close to executing it.

She wriggled away and stood on her own, facing Auntie and Scarlett, Freddy at her side. Auntie looked slightly hurt. Scarlett didn't seem to notice; she was focused on Freddy.

Scarlett's hazel eyes narrowed. "Who's he?"

Maya stepped closer to Freddy. A shadow of sadness, of dislike, flickered across Scarlett's face.

"He's Freddy."

The tension in the air climbed higher and higher. It was almost at its peak. Almost, almost—

"Okay," Auntie interrupted, her voice jarring like an axe. "Maya, we are so happy to see you. I can't believe it—at last—" Tears reemerged on her face, and Maya forced a smile.

"Let's save the arguing for another day," Auntie continued. "Please? But Maya, I would very much like to know your story. Tell us, and then we'll tell you ours."

Maya nodded and began. She told them about her escapades all over time and then her eventual arrival at 15 Harding Street. She explained how she'd been hit by a bike and ended up in London in the 1910s, though she was careful to avoid any mention of how difficult time travel had been, and how she had seemed have lost that ability altogether. There was no reason Auntie and Scarlett needed to know that, she told herself, embarrassed.

She talked about Mrs. Attleboro's orphanage, how she'd met Freddy and how he'd believed her when she told him about the prophecy, about the OCT.

Maya ended with the fight against the OCT—for the octagon on their cloaks had assured her that it was the OCT—how she'd snuck out the window, how she'd hidden in the dead end before going forward to fight them. She was a fine storyteller, but her words were abrasive, like sandpaper. Maya was aware of this, though whether that was due to the fact that English had rubbed off on her, or she hadn't spoken Cloudian in so long, or something else entirely, she didn't know.

Auntie smiled tearily as Maya recounted her journey, but she didn't draw any nearer to her because if Maya's voice was like sandpaper, then her body was the stiff wood being sanded.

"But what about you?" Maya asked. "Where have you been?"

Now it was Scarlett and Auntie's turn to tell their story, though they did so in turns, practically finishing each other's sentences. Maya stiffened further at this, and when Scarlett called Aunt Flora "Auntie," Maya nearly tipped over and fell into the grasses below. Scarlett blushed slightly and continued speaking.

Finally, it came time to explain how they had arrived at 15 Harding Street just after Maya had left.

"You weren't there," Auntie explained, "and we didn't know what to do. All of this time, we'd been searching for you, and we were sure that we would find you, but all that we found was this." From within her pocket, she pulled out a golden chain. And on the end was a necklace with a dove engraved on the front and an address engraved on the back.

Maya gasped slightly and rushed forward. Her eyes sparkled as she took the necklace in her hands, holding it delicately, carefully, as if it could blow away in a breeze. "Thank you," she whispered reverently.

Auntie said, "You're welcome," but all she could think of was the fact that this, not their reunion, was the happiest they had seen Maya yet.

As Maya clasped the necklace around her neck, Freddy coughed. It wasn't a real cough, but it got everyone's attention.

"Um," he stuttered, looking shocked at having three people who lived in the clouds staring at him. "What do we do now?" Scarlett scoffed at this, but didn't respond, so Freddy's English words dropped to the ground, buried in the grasses, and for a moment, no one was brave enough to pick them up.

Finally, after shooting Scarlett a "get along" look, Auntie said, "Well, Maya, you think you are the one in the prophecy, right?"

"I know I am." Maya spoke through gritted teeth.

"Right, of course." Auntie looked a little taken aback. "We came to that conclusion too after we almost found you by the lakeside. It was clearly the OCT who were there. And certainly, after the events of earlier this morning . . . I think it's highly probable."

Maya and Freddy exchanged looks. "More than 'highly,'" Maya muttered. She was bored now. While it was great to see Auntie and Scarlett again—and it really was—she was ready to get on her way. She and Freddy had a plan, and they needed to carry it out. They didn't need Auntie and Scarlett to help with that.

"We'll need a plan of action," Auntie was saying. She paced back and forth, the grasses nipping at her ankles, a predawn light cast on her weathered face.

"We need a plan of action?" Maya countered. "If I recall, I said I was the one in the prophecy, and it looks like I am. Maybe you all should just trust my judgement."

Scarlett and Auntie recoiled, alarmed at the snake that had lashed out from inside Maya's mouth. Maya herself winced. She hadn't meant to be that cruel, only to let the serpent play a little bit. What she'd said was true, after all.

"Maya," Auntie said in Cloudian, her voice steely—Maya was reminded of that supper on their porch back in the Land of the Clouds, the last time she had lashed out—"we are coming with you, whether you like it or not."

Maya found herself avoiding Auntie's gaze out of

habit. "You may think that you are the only one here who has seen hardships on Earth, the only one who's had any trouble. You're wrong, do you know that? The police were going to come to Earth to look for you. Not us." At this, Maya hesitantly looked into Auntie's face. It was carved out of marble. "But I told the police officer that you would come more willingly if I came to find you, and I think that was the right choice. At any rate, we aren't supposed to have stayed on Earth. As soon as we found you, we were supposed to return to the Land. All three of us. And yet here we are. Scarlett and I aren't showing any sign of wanting to go back there, are we? Because we believe you, whether you want that or not, and we are willing to openly disobey the police in order to help you. Think about that the next time you want to get mad, okay?"

Maya sighed. "Fine." The sound was like spit hurled out of her mouth.

"Now we need a plan," Auntie said, this time in English, her voice still eerily calm.

Maya didn't retort this time, though her tongue itched to. For now, she was willing to assume the pretense of friendliness—just until she could ditch Scarlett and Auntie and finish her mission alone with Freddy. They didn't believe she was the one—she would show them.

"I think we should take our time," Auntie said. Her voice was braced in expectation of a shot fired from Maya. Nothing came. "We don't even know where to go. Maya, I know you think 15 Harding Street holds all the answers, but we can't be sure of that. Besides, they know you'll go there."

"Maybe we could find the OCT's stronghold and breach it," Scarlett suggested.

Maya had never felt such loathing toward her friend. *The OCT's stronghold.* 15 Harding Street was the answer; she was sure of it. She had to bite her lip to dam up the river of attacks that wanted to flow forth.

"Fine," she spat out again. "I guess that's fine for now."

Freddy coughed, and once again, everyone's eyes flicked to him. He swallowed. "How will we find the stronghold?"

Auntie nodded thoughtfully. "Good question. I'm sure we can figure it out. There are a lot of records about the OCT back in the Land. I've read a bunch of them. I'm sure I can remember something. For now, though, we'd better keep on our feet. The OCT were able to track Maya before, and I'm sure that they can do it again. We'll need to time travel often. Maya, are you up to that?"

Maya nodded shortly, ignoring the glance that Freddy threw at her. Auntie and Scarlett could find out some other time.

Scarlett frowned slightly, narrowed her eyes at Freddy, then tugged on Auntie's sleeve to exchange a few whispered words with her. Maya rolled her eyes.

A few seconds later, they turned back. Maya's eyes glinted coldly, no longer harboring warmth in their metallic specks, but iciness.

"What were you talking about?" Maya asked, her voice still carrying the sediment of the English language. The question had a barb at the end, and she knew it.

"Scarlett suggested that we go back to the cave we've been sheltering in. It isn't too far," Auntie replied coolly, in English again.

Maya's eyes probed her friend, searching for a lie, but Scarlett revealed nothing. "Sounds good. For now."

Auntie nodded. "That's what I thought. Now, we'd best get there before the sun is fully up. We don't want anyone to find us standing here."

Auntie grabbed Scarlett's arm, and Scarlett reached over and clutched Maya, and Maya grabbed Freddy and away they went, teleporting across the land as the sun rose, soft and pink, beyond the green hills.

CHAPTER 8

The Cave

When they finally reached the cave, the sun was still just coming up, appearing to light the world on fire. Though Maya, Auntie, and Scarlett weren't shivering in their tunics, Freddy quivered in the early morning air.

Auntie led the group single file up a hill full of large boulders. They scrambled over rocks, their palms chafing on the rough surfaces. Panting, they climbed further up, until the summit, which appeared to be relatively flat, was almost within reach.

Maya would have liked to have gone to the top of the hill and looked out to see all there was to see. She vaguely wondered whether they were near Shellside. Subconsciously, her hand raised to her chest, she fingered the necklace. Relief blew through her, calm and cooling. It was still there. It hadn't disappeared again or vanished into thin air.

Suddenly, Auntie turned sharply, causing Maya to bump into her. Maya muttered an apology, but Auntie either didn't hear or didn't acknowledge it. She was still walking, heading down a narrow ravine walled in by sheer rock on both sides. Pebbles lined the ravine, getting stuck in Maya's shoes. "Ouch," she mumbled again and again as they stabbed her feet. Auntie, along with everyone else, was still silent.

As they came to the end of the ravine, the dawn light, which was leaving tall shadows on the walls, nearly disappeared altogether—it was all dark, in shadow. Maya had to squint in order to see anything as Auntie entered a mouth-like hole at the end of the ravine.

And then, as she entered it as well, the darkness seemed to fall away a little bit. Maya was in a cave, large and round. However, unlike most caves, she realized, this had another entrance, another gaping mouth.

Maya ran over to the second entrance, where light streamed in. She looked down. A straight wall of rock met her eyes. Maya turned back to face Auntie. "It's on the edge of a cliff?" Her voice seemed to shatter the silence, turning it to glass shards on the floor.

Auntie nodded. "It's a perfect location. This way, we can see if anyone's coming, and there's always a second way to escape."

Maya gave a begrudgingly appraising look. As much as she hated being here, for it meant that she could not immediately hunt the OCT, it wasn't a bad place to be.

"Um, excuse me," Freddy said. He was standing in the middle of the cave, next to the remains of a campfire. "Could you talk in English? Or German?"

"Of course," Auntie replied in English.

"What are we going to do now?" Scarlett interjected in Cloudian.

Auntie shot her a visible "get along" look, and Scarlett repeated her sentence in English.

"Well, I would say that we should have breakfast, but our provisions are low and we need to ration," Auntie said.

Maya leaned against one of the sloped cave walls. It was slightly uncomfortable, but not unbearably so; besides, doing so gave off just the right air of carelessness. "Can't we just go out somewhere to pick up food? You've got money, right?"

Auntie pursed her lips. "No. The whole point of hiding is to stay hidden. We mustn't go out to get food until we run out."

Maya huffed. Freddy's eyes darted around, as if unsure whose side he should take. In the end, he snuck over to Maya's.

"For now," Auntie continued, "let's think. Where could the OCT stronghold be?"

Maya opened her mouth, but Auntie cut her off. "I'm not ruling out 15 Harding Street," she said tiredly, "but we need to think of other possibilities as well."

Maya scowled. "Fine. Have it your way. But when I'm right—"

"Maya!" Auntie's eyes were a strikingly powerful cobalt blue. "I'm not sure what's changed since we last saw you in the Land, but we love you and want to help you. You're not getting rid of me and Scarlett—"

"I wish," muttered Maya.

"—so you just need to put up with that, okay? What would be even better," she added, "would be if you could get also along with us, but maybe that's too much to ask."

Maya drew a sharp breath. Auntie had never, ever spoken to her like that. *Well, two can play that game.*

"Fine, Flora." Maya made the last word sound as ugly as possible, as un-flowery as she could.

Auntie stiffened. "Well, I'm glad we've got that settled," she said. "Now, how about we all get some sleep. I know it's morning, but we could all use some time to decompress. I'll take watch. You kids get some rest."

Maya inhaled quietly and released her breath softly. There was no use arguing. It was better to save her energy for when she really needed to get her way. "I don't have a blanket or anything," she told Auntie, trying to keep her voice cool. Instead, it came out icy.

"Use my cloak." Auntie paused. "Don't you have a bag or something?"

"Lost it."

"Ah. Oh, wait, I have something for you . . ."

Maya perked up. "

Auntie withdrew a short scabbard from her bag and placed it in Maya's hands. "Your dagger."

"My dagger?"

"You left it at home when you came here."

"Oh, well. Thanks." Maya put the dagger on the ground, laid Auntie's cloak out, and sat down on it. She stretched out and lay on her side, ready to fall asleep.

Next to her, Freddy was quiet. He didn't have a blanket or anything, Maya noticed, and he was still shivering. Sighing, she stood up, stepped off of the cloak, and pulled it up off the floor. She draped it over Freddy, and then lay back down, staring at each crevice and dent in the cave wall, imagining ancient humans who could have lived in this very spot, who could have stared up at these same walls. There were no caves like this—centuries old, rich with the past—in the Land of the Clouds; there were no caves at all. Sometimes, Maya thought, as her eyes began to close—though she could have sworn she wasn't tired—Earth still managed to impress her.

Auntie sat near the remains of the campfire, dagger by her side. She gazed out across the cave, her eyes sliding from one sleeping child to the next. Maya was by the entrance that dropped over the cliff face. She rolled over in her sleep, and Auntie saw her face. It seemed so much younger, so much fuller. It wasn't taut or scowling, consumed with conflict, but peaceful. She hadn't seen Maya look so tranquil in a long time.

Freddy lay near Maya, Auntie's cloak cocooning him in its soft warmth. That boy was interesting. As passive as he sometimes appeared, Auntie had seen his eyes—those magnificent, fading eyes—gleam with a hunger to prove himself. He and Maya were so alike. Auntie wondered whether, in their current circumstances, Maya would have lent a cloak to anyone else.

Lastly there was Scarlett, resting on the other side of the cave in a corner close to the ravine entrance. Her hair fell like a curtain over her face, but Auntie could still make out the hint of a frown on her features. She had protested Auntie taking watch after the others had fallen asleep, but Auntie had shooed her off.

She wondered why Scarlett didn't trust Freddy. Auntie herself certainly thought the boy was slightly odd, but there wasn't anything wrong with him.

Auntie sat in silence, listening to the slow breath of the children. The sun had fully risen, and bright light came in over the cliff face. Birds chirped outside in the spring air, flying past the cave every so often.

The cave was secluded, Auntie thought. That was why she and Scarlett had chosen it in the first place. Well, that and it wasn't too far from Shellside; after Maya had vanished on Harding Street, they hadn't had the energy to go very far away. However, Auntie figured it was a good idea not to mention the cave's proximity to the town to Maya. It would only fire her up.

Auntie wasn't very worried about being found, not at the moment, anyway, since the cave was well hidden. She let her guard down a bit and began to relax.

Maya and Scarlett woke up with simultaneous gasps. In both their eyes, there was a wild, panicked look. Auntie scrambled to her feet. "What happened?"

Now Freddy had stirred, awakened by the sudden noise. He rushed to get up, shoving the cloak away. "Wha-

wha—?" he stammered.

Scarlett ignored him, and before Maya could start, began speaking. "My power," she said, out of breath. "I saw the orphanage. It burned."

"Like what you saw before," Auntie said steadily, "with the necklace."

The other two were not nearly so calm.

"It burned?!" Freddy cried.

"Your power?" Maya exclaimed, glaring alternately at Auntie and Scarlett. "Your power? Your power doesn't work in dreams, does it?"

Scarlett glanced nervously at Auntie. Maya, observing the interaction, stood up and began pacing. "It does! It does! But you never told me! Why would you never tell me?" She was dripping with incredulity.

"I'm sorry," Scarlett said. "But now you know."

Maya scoffed, but forced herself to swallow her anger, to save it up for later. "Anyway . . . the orphanage burned?"

"Yes. The OCT burned it down."

"Was anyone . . . hurt?" Freddy asked.

"No. Everyone was already outside. But the flames— they were astonishing. Sky high. I wouldn't be surprised if half of Taleo Place burned down."

"So, the OCT must be furious, then," Maya said. "Really furious."

"Yes," Scarlett affirmed. "We need to be careful."

Auntie fired a look at Maya that seemed to say, "See, I told you you'd want help." Maya didn't respond.

"Maya, what did you see?" Scarlett asked.

"Nothing. It was just a dream." But it hadn't been just a dream. It had been the dream, the first time she'd had it in a long time. She'd felt so vulnerable, so unprotected as she'd sat on the grass watching the sky become clouded, feeling her mother clasp the necklace around her neck. But she could never tell any of this to anyone now. Except Freddy. She would tell Freddy.

Auntie stared at Maya for a second, as if trying to examine her with X-ray vision, to see whatever was hidden in her mind. Maya stood defiantly still, and Auntie looked away.

"Well," Auntie said. "Now you're awake, maybe we ought to start thinking about what our plan is from here on out."

"I've got a few ideas about where the stronghold might be, and with our teleporter and time travel, they shouldn't be too hard to find," Scarlett piped up.

Scarlett moved closer and began speaking to Auntie.

"Are you two going to join us?" Auntie asked.

"We'll come in a minute," Maya said, smiling falsely. She sat down beside Freddy and began telling him about her dream.

"But then stupid Scarlett with her stupid powers," she grumbled afterward. "It's not fair that she has hers and I don't. Especially because I am the one in the prophecy. You'd think that I would know how I'm going to defeat the OCT by now."

"It is," Freddy said. "But I'm sure you'll find your power soon. You're much better than Scarlett."

Maya allowed herself a real smile. "I think I'm a lot better than everybody." She was only half joking.

They sat in silence for a moment. Maya glanced out of the cave. She could see green fields in the distance, occasionally lined with wooden fences. The sky above was a clear blue with no clouds in sight. If Maya thought hard enough, she could almost imagine that she was in the Land of the Clouds. The idea was unsettling. She wasn't sure why.

As she gazed out into the distance, she caught sight of small black figures marching toward them from the horizon. She squinted even harder, her stomach turning unpleasantly. Who were they?

Freddy, who couldn't see the figures, asked, "Who'd you say that the leader of the OCT was, again?"

Maya was hardly focused on the question. "Um . . . something von Hopsburg, I think."

"Von Hopsburg," Freddy repeated. "Sounds evil."

"Yeah . . ." Maya was still watching the figures, who were growing steadily closer. She could make out eight of them, each in a black robe. "Flora," she said, "I think they're coming. The OCT." She grabbed her sheathed dagger and hooked it onto her belt.

Scarlett and Auntie rushed over to Maya and looked out across the fields. "That's them." Auntie said. "We need to go."

"Teleporting or time travel?" Scarlett asked.

"Time travel. Teleporting won't be fast enough."

Maya felt a rock, one of the boulders on the hill, perhaps, fall into her stomach. She squirmed slightly.

"Maya," Auntie was saying, "you take Freddy, all right? Scarlett will come with me. There's a time with a market just outside the cave, which you'll find in the Tunnel. We'll meet you there."

Anger boiled up inside Maya. *Stupid . . . time travel . . . can't even . . .*

"No," Maya said.

"No?" repeated Auntie incredulously. "Now isn't the time to argue, Maya—let's go!"

"No. I can't," Maya said her through gritted teeth, still watching the advancing figures. She was so close to spilling over the top, so close to letting it all out.

"What do you mean you can't?" Auntie placed a hand on Maya's shoulder, trying to get Maya to face her.

Maya swatted the hand off, stood up, and whirled

around. "I can't!" she roared. "I can't time travel!" Tears should have gushed from Maya's eyes, but they didn't. She felt dry, as arid as a desert and burning with rage.

"You can't time travel?!" Auntie burst out, clearly annoyed that this information had been withheld.

"No. I can't," Maya growled.

"Since when?"

"15 Harding Street. Will you stop interrogating me? We need to go!" Maya yelled, her hair whipping crazily around her head.

"Yes, we'll go," Auntie said. "But we need to talk about this."

"No, we don't!"

"Yes, we do!" Auntie shouted. "Everyone, grab my sleeve. I'll just have to time travel with all of you."

They all held on tight, Maya pinching Auntie's skin, and, as the figures drew ever closer, they disappeared into Auntie's faded meadow, evading the OCT yet again.

CHAPTER 9

Splitting Up

Maya frowned as Auntie led the group through the faded meadow. She would've sighed—she tried to sigh—but the air swept the sound up, and it dissolved into nothingness.

She wanted to let go of Auntie's sleeve. How cruel was it that the second she admitted that she couldn't time travel, she was forced to travel through someone else's Tunnel of Time? But if she let go, what would happen? Auntie was forcing her way through long grasses now. Would Maya simply be swallowed by the grasses, simply not exist anymore? She almost considered testing her theory, if not just to spite her companions, but then she caught Freddy's eye.

He seemed to be reading her mind. "Don't do it. We've still got to defeat the OCT," he seemed to be saying.

Right, she reminded herself. *Right. Hold on.* Soon, so soon, she would get her answers.

Auntie was now leading the group through a hedge maze. As they walked—well, jogged—Maya made out hazy images against the sides of the maze. Was this the tunnel? Why weren't the images clear?

They stopped abruptly in the path. Auntie took a deep breath and then pushed her arms through a hazy image of the cave. Long grasses picked the four of them up, and suddenly they were being carried back through the meadow. Maya writhed and squirmed, irked by how uncomfortable, how prickly this method of travel was. She glanced at Freddy. He seemed to be having the same problem. Scarlett and Auntie, however, appeared to be perfectly at ease.

Before she knew it, though, they were back where they had started, in the clearing. Auntie closed her eyes. They were traveling up, up. The clearing, the meadow began to vanish, and then ...

Maya was sprawled on her back on the cold floor of the cave. Stretching, for she felt achy now, she sat up and looked around.

The cave appeared to be exactly same. "Did it work?" she asked no one in particular.

"Yes," Auntie said. "It did."

Maya turned her head to where Auntie's voice was coming from. She and Scarlett were already on their feet— perhaps they had stayed standing the whole time. But Freddy was in a similar position to Maya.

Freddy tilted his head. "What's that noise?"

Maya tilted her head too, then stood up, brushed dust and dirt off of her tunic, and walked over to the opening of the cave, the one that led out over the cliff face. Below, in the same place that the OCT had stood just seconds before, there was the market Auntie had mentioned.

Tents lined the field that used to stand empty. Though they looked miniature from this height, Maya could see throngs of people making their way to see different vendors. There were hundreds of them, all piled together. Maya's eyes were wide with excitement. She felt a buzz in her chest that had nothing to do with the OCT, with the prophecy. No, this was lighter, more pleasant.

Maya turned around. Freddy, Auntie, and Scarlett had come to join her. "I want to go there," she told them. It was more than that, she knew. She *needed* to go there. She needed to feel all of that energy, needed to absorb the liveliness that resided below.

"No," Auntie said, not taking her eyes off the market.

The word registered in Maya's ears, and it was as if a wave had crashed down, a wave that she had been holding back. "What?" Maya asked, her voice like a steel bar.

"We—you—are *not* going to the market," Auntie repeated. She stepped away from the opening and back into the depths of the cave.

"What do you mean 'we're not going'? Why can't we?" Maya's voice was rich with indignation.

Auntie's voice grew harder and colder. "Maya, we barely escaped from the OCT just a few minutes ago. With our luck, they probably already know that we're here. Have you considered *they might be waiting for you at the market?*"

"Even better," Maya retorted. "We'll finally get to actually do something."

"You don't understand," Auntie said. "You haven't fought them before. You don't know what they're like. I was in the war . . ."

"In case you're forgetting," Maya shot back, her voice gaining heat, "I have fought them before—"

"—And you needed our help."

"Because *you* dragged me away!"

The tension in the room was a mountain growing taller and taller, and Maya and Auntie kept climbing further up. Scarlett and Freddy watched from the ground, amazed at this display of animosity.

"Did it ever occur to you," Maya yelled, "that Freddy and I had a plan?"

Scarlett glared at Freddy, who tried his best to stand tall.

"We were going to run away the next day. We had everything all worked out! And then you came in and ruined it all!" The specks in Maya's eyes glowed like they were on fire.

"We saved your lives!" Auntie countered. She wasn't shouting, but her voice carried the same punch.

It was too late, though. Maya was on a rampage. "We would've been fine on our own." Then she turned the anger onto herself. "How could I let you take us away? How? How? And then, just now—I saw the OCT, and what did I do? I told you. I don't know why. It would've been better to let them come. Then we could've fought. We could've made a move. But I was so stupid. I was foolish enough to trust you, to believe that you would actually believe in me. But you don't." Auntie's eyes were watering as Maya pulled out the last weapon, the deadly weapon. Her favorite weapon. "You had parents. I don't. So don't you dare try to understand, because you never will." Her voice had grown quiet as she twisted the blade into Auntie's heart. She turned on her heel, feeling aflame with anger. "I'm going to save the world. Goodbye."

Maya stood by the mouth of the cave, the one that led to the ravine. Then she turned to face the cave one more time. Auntie opened her mouth to speak, but Maya's eyes were focused on only one person. "Freddy, let's go." She didn't sound mad when she spoke to him. He nodded and ran over to join Maya. Together, they turned their backs on Scarlett and Auntie and marched away.

If the tension in the cave had been loud, the silence afterward was louder. Auntie sank to the ground, shuddering with silent sobs. Scarlett ran over to comfort her and kneeled down, her hazel eyes soft and kind. "It's okay, Auntie. It's okay."

Auntie looked up. Her eyes were red and puffy, but dry for the moment. She took a shaky breath and straightened up.

"I'm sure Maya didn't mean it. She'll come around."

But Auntie shook her head. "No." Her voice was clear, not stuffy or teary. "She meant every word."

Scarlett leaned back. "But she couldn't have. I mean, what she said was..."

Auntie rubbed her face thoughtfully. "She meant it. I know she did."

"And you're okay with that?" Their voices seemed small, merely sitting in the shadow that Maya had left behind. "She was—"

"—angrier than she's ever been," Auntie finished. "And no, I'm not okay with it. But what can I do?" A sense of helplessness was drowning Auntie.

Scarlett was silent for a moment. "This is worse than when she left. I told you, remember? I told you what she'd been like on that afternoon when she decided that she was the one. It was scary the way she put herself in those shoes. This is by far worse."

They were quiet again for a few minutes, and then Auntie spoke, rallying all of her determination, all of her courage, pouring them out in these words: "This doesn't mean that we have to give up, though. I'm not letting anything bad happen to Maya, as little as she may want my help."

The words sat in the air for a few seconds. Hanging off of them was the unspoken sentence "Maybe we'll convince her to come back."

Scarlett swallowed. "I bet we could guess where they're going to go now."

Auntie mustered a small laugh. "Yeah." She looked out over the cliff face at the crowds that teemed below.

Maya and Freddy scrambled over the boulders that lined the hillside as they made their way down toward the market. The air was mild and sweet, a perfect summer day. There was hardly a breeze, and barely any clouds in the sky. Maya felt free, freer than she ever had before. It seemed her anger had morphed, her intensity had been poured into some other emotion—confidence.

She had done it. She had broken free, and now she was finally getting closer to her goal of completing the prophecy, of beating the OCT. Maya laughed. It felt good to laugh. Freddy looked at her and smiled.

"We're getting there," she said to him. "We are going to defeat the OCT, just like the prophecy says."

His grin became wider. "Yes, we are."

"Oh, so how was time traveling for you?" she asked. They were now at the foot of the hill, walking in the luscious green grass.

Freddy paused for a moment. "It was weird. But I'm not dead or anything, so that's good, I guess."

Maya laughed. "That is good."

"Where are we going anyway?"

"To the market!" Maya's eyes were bright and sparkling. "I want to see all there is to see. And then we'll think about where we're going to go. Because it is up to us to defeat the OCT."

Freddy smiled.

"I wonder when we are," Maya mused, as they drew closer and closer to the market.

Freddy gave her a quizzical look.

"Well, we time traveled. So, we're not in 1910 anymore."

Freddy's eyes grew wide. "That's so cool!"

Maya gave him an offhand glance. "Yeah, I know."

"But, I mean, it's different for you because you're not human. But me, I never, ever, ever dreamed that I would actually time travel. I mean," he rambled on, "I've *thought* about it, of course, but to actually time travel . . ."

Maya laughed. It felt so nice to be free of Auntie, of Scarlett. Maya thought briefly of her best friend. Or maybe ex-best friend. What had changed? Or had they just never really gotten along to begin with? A hissing voice in Maya's head said it was the latter, and Maya was willing to believe that, but somewhere else inside her mind there was a different whisper. *It's your fault. You drove her away. It's your fault . . . your fault.*

Maya twitched and shrugged her shoulders, trying to shake the voice off. "Go away," she muttered.

Freddy looked at her. "Me?"

"No, not you . . . Never mind."

The market loomed before them. Up close, they could smell fresh bread, buttery popcorn, even cotton candy being spun. Maya's stomach rumbled hungrily. People were smiling and laughing, holding each other's hands, calling after small children for them not to stray too far.

Maya wondered vaguely why there was a market set up in the middle of a field where there was no town in sight, but these thoughts vanished as they began to walk past different booths.

Multicolored tents lined the paths of beaten-down grass. Each booth cast a shadow, a cool haven that felt refreshing and rejuvenating. Maya and Freddy peered at the goods lined up on tables, pretty little necklaces or honey or fresh fruit. Their mouths watered as they passed a stand full of chocolates whose delicious scent permeated the air. Maya wished more than anything that she had some money in her pocket.

There were some pets in the market, dogs on leashes, sniffing the ground diligently in front of their owners, soaking up all of the rich smells. There was a pen of farm animals too, at the north end of the market. Maya and Freddy made their way over, where a crowd of kids were perched on the fences, stretching their hands out to pet the goats within. A few parents hung back, chatting with other adults, cold drinks in their hands.

One of the children had a small black dog on a leash. Her tail wagging profusely, the puppy growled at the goats. Maya and Freddy stifled laughs. Then the dog barked. It seemed like it was supposed to be a threatening bark, but instead it seemed childish, slightly panicked. Then the dog made a run for it, sprinting away from the goat pen as fast as her little legs would carry her. The kid holding the leash, a young boy in shorts and a blue T-shirt, dropped it in surprise, and the dog bolted, tearing toward the stalls, her leash trailing after her.

The boy sighed. "Freya, come back here!" he called and began to run after the dog. The other children, including Maya and Freddy, grinned and laughed as the sun shone down merry and bright.

Auntie and Scarlett, staring out at the market, watched as two kids, one with long brown hair and the other with short, flaming-red hair, made their way toward the market.

"You were right," Scarlett said.

"Well, it wasn't very hard to guess, was it? Besides, since Maya can't time travel, they can't really go anywhere."

"Yeah . . . but you never told her that this cave is close to Shellside?"

"No, I didn't," Auntie said confidently. That clearly had been the right choice, seeing as Maya was on a reckless streak. "I still can't believe that they're actually going to the market . . ."

"Are we going after them?"

Auntie pondered this. What chance did they have of actually convincing Maya to rejoin them? And yet, if Auntie knew one thing, it was that she wasn't going to let Maya go at this alone. "Yes," she said desperately. "We're going after them. I don't know what's going to happen, but we'll take it as it comes."

And with that, they left the cool dampness of the cave and followed in Maya and Freddy's footsteps.

CHAPTER 10

At the Market

A untie and Scarlett raced toward the tents and carts that made up the market.

"Are you sure that Maya's going to come back?" Scarlett asked tentatively. "I mean, she was really mad . . ."

"I know, I know," Auntie said, her voice reeking of preemptive defeat. "She probably won't come back. You know her. When has anyone told her to do anything that she actually ended up doing? Or at least if she does come back, it won't be because we've asked."

Scarlett nodded as they both began to slow, the market growing ever closer.

"There are so many things . . . so many people . . ."

The market didn't have the same effect on Auntie, who was staring distractedly through the rows of tents, looking not at the delicate glass jewelry that glinted in the sun nor the clothes made of soft fabric, which waved mesmerizingly in puffs of wind, but into the space beyond them. Into the space where Maya could've been.

"How are we ever going to find them?" Auntie whispered, mostly to herself. North didn't just disappear; even when you couldn't find it, it was always there. Maya had to be here in this market, in some place where Auntie and Scarlett could find her.

"When Maya said she couldn't time travel," Scarlett asked quietly, for there were people passing by, "what did she mean? Did that mean that she was like me, how I can't time travel?"

Auntie had perked up at Maya's name and now pulled

Scarlett aside, between the canvas walls of two tents, away from the rushing passersby, to explain.

"I think she wore herself out. I mean, I think that if you tried to time travel again, you would be able to. From what Maya told us, she did a lot of time traveling. It's not at all surprising that she can't do it anymore."

Scarlett opened her mouth to ask another question, but Auntie interrupted her.

"She'll be able to time travel again. At some point." The words hurt Auntie to say. "That was your question, though, right?"

"Yeah . . ." Scarlett's gaze drifted to the sliver of sky between the walls of tents as she leaned back against the rough canvas wall. "And then there's that Freddy—"

At the same time, Auntie said, "Of course, it could've been more than that—"

They paused and looked at each other. "You go first," they said in unison. They paused again. Auntie took advantage of the silence.

"I just think that it could've been something else, something in addition, that caused Maya to lose her ability to time travel. She said that she got hit with a bicycle. I don't think that was an accident. Someone deliberately ran into her, and then she fell through time, and all the way to London." Auntie stopped for a second, collecting her thoughts. "It is entirely possible that Maya was just so frail at that point that, when hit, she just lost her grip on the world. But I also think that maybe the person who hit her knew where she would end up, wanted her to end up there."

"You think that the OCT hit Maya?" Scarlett hissed incredulously, looking nervously around.

"Yes." Auntie took a deep breath. "I mean, we know that they were onto her from the beginning. They'd been following her. When she got hit, if the cyclist was from the OCT, then it couldn't have been by her own doing that Maya ended up where she did. The OCT know a lot of powerful magic that has long been forgotten in the Land of the Clouds."

Scarlett was gaping.

Auntie nodded. "There are a lot of secrets that have been lost to time in the Land. But my point is that the OCT could certainly have been capable of making sure that Maya ended up in London in 1910, and also could have somehow blocked her ability to time travel." Auntie spoke the last few words very carefully, as if she knew she was treading a dangerous path, forging a way through hidden land mines.

Scarlett looked as if a land mine had already caught her. "What?" She was whispering as loud as she could. "They can do that?"

Auntie nodded gravely and then spoke again. "I'm sure it won't be long until they know we're here, that Maya is here. We need to find her."

"We could go up there," Scarlett said, pointing up to the crack of sky between the tents, just as the vague din around them grew louder, as more shoppers flowed into the tents on either side of them.

"On the top of the tent?"

"Yeah. I bet we can see all of the market from up there."

"Sure. Worth a shot." Auntie clutched the side of the tent and began to climb lightly up as though she were a spider. Scarlett followed, though with a little less grace.

Up the sloping roof of the tent they went, up to the very top, where they squatted down, carefully balanced. Together, the pair of them peered out over the market, absorbing the rows of tents that stretched out for what seemed like forever.

"I don't think they're here," Scarlett said after a minute.

Auntie made no sign that she had heard. Instead, she continued looking out over the market, her eyes sliding back and forth like sweeping searchlights.

"Auntie, come on," Scarlett said, beginning to inch down the side of the tent. "Someone's going to see us, and then people will ask questions." It was true that a few passersby, their arms laden with souvenirs and goods, had glimpsed them perched on top of the tent and cast suspicious looks.

"No. Wait." Auntie searched the area even more intently than before. She had seen something, she thought. *Where was it? Where was it? There.*

Auntie inhaled sharply, as though her breath was stabbing her. "No, no, no," she muttered.

"What?" Scarlett asked, clambering back up next to Auntie. "Is it Maya?"

"No. Worse." Auntie pointed her finger toward the west part of the market. It was an accusation, a threat. "Look right past the red tent."

Scarlett followed her finger. "Oh no."

There, standing at the entrance of a beige tent selling various whirligigs, were eight figures, tall and cloaked. The shoppers who bustled around them seemed to fear their presence, hunching over, clutching their children's hands when they passed them.

"It only makes sense that they're here, though," Auntie said, sighing. Her voice was dry, a desert.

"Well," Scarlett admitted, "now we need to find Maya."

Auntie nodded, and they sat in silence, gazing out at the market, at the shoppers with their light hearts as their own grew more weighted by the second.

"Aha!" Scarlett said.

"Do you see them?" Auntie sounded like a small child

filled with naive hope.

"I think so . . ." Something in her voice was hesitant.

"Where? Where?" Auntie practically begged.

"They're over by the animal pen." Scarlett nodded in the general direction. "Where that little dog just ran away," she added.

Auntie's eyes lit up as she found the place. "Come on. Let's go."

They climbed as quickly as they could down to the ground and burst out from between the two tents. Auntie ran down the grassy paths of the market, dodging shoppers and little kids, completely oblivious to the aromas and cool crafts beaming from within the shops.

She looked back; Scarlett had stopped at a tent full of framed prints.

"Come on! We've got to find Maya and Freddy!" Auntie called. *Why was Scarlett stopping?*

Her companion sighed and began running again, though Auntie could tell by the furrow in her brow that she was deep in thought. Then once again, she stopped.

Auntie blew out an exasperated sigh. "Come. On."

"No, there's something about Freddy. He's weird. I don't know if it's because he's human, but there's something . . ." Scarlett muttered as Auntie grabbed her arm.

"We're not talking about Freddy," Auntie reminded her. "And I'm sure he's fine." Though she didn't say it, she thought she knew what was bothering Scarlett. Losing her best friend, especially to a little human, was tough. Maybe Scarlett wouldn't admit it right now, but Auntie was sure that was the problem. So she ignored Scarlett and dragged her over to the animal pen.

Auntie stopped in her tracks. There she was. Standing, just a few yards away, staring at the animal pen, a red-headed boy by her side. Maya. North.

Scarlett shook Auntie's hand off and together they watched, silent, for a moment, déjà vu coursing through her veins like poison. How many times had they been this close to Maya? How many times had she vanished just as they were about to call out? How many times had she been in danger, so much danger, and they had been unable to help?

Danger. The word sparked a flame in Auntie's mind, and she began to move forward. The OCT was here, in the market. *Danger.*

And suddenly the two of them were standing just behind Maya and Freddy, who were still unaware of their presence. Maya's shoulders were less tense than they had been in the cave, and her neck was less rigid. She was relaxed, Auntie realized. Well, maybe not relaxed, for she still seemed slightly on guard, but more so than before.

Auntie coughed. The sound was small and meek, and Maya whirled around, her eyes blazing, her shoulders taut. Freddy turned around as well, his eyes immediately penetrating, though not nearly as intensely as Maya's.

"Maya," Auntie said tentatively. What should she say next? What would convince Maya to come back to her? "We can help you." There. That was a start. Auntie watched for a glimpse of softness in Maya's rock-hard eyes, a glimpse of compassion.

"I don't need you." The words were a steel beam.

"But Maya . . ." Auntie protested, as Maya's glare flickered from Auntie to Scarlett and back again.

"What makes you think I want your help?" she hissed, her words fiery and sharp.

"We care about you. We want to help you." Auntie was melting, an ice cube under Maya's heat.

"I don't care." Maya started laughing mad, crazy laughter. She began to storm away, Freddy following.

Auntie and Scarlett rushed to keep up with them. "Maya, please. Don't turn us away."

Maya scoffed.

"You're in danger," Auntie cried, tears filling her eyes, creeping down her face. North couldn't run away. North couldn't just decide to stop being North.

Maya stopped abruptly and turned on her heel, facing her aunt. "I know I'm in danger. But I'm the one in the prophecy. I can handle it."

"What if you can't?" Scarlett blurted out. "You're eleven years old, for crying out loud! You're not an adult!"

"You're eleven too!" Maya retorted.

"Yes, but I'm not risking my neck without thinking. I'm not blindly wandering into dangerous places!"

"So what if I am?! Maybe I'm just better than you. I've always been better than you."

No one answered. And then Auntie, wiping her face and blinking back tears, said, "Maya, the OCT are here. They're looking for you. They want to harm you." Her voice was worn, but strong.

"Good." It was frightening the way Maya looked, so small in stature yet talking as if she were a giant. "Let them come. Then they can lead us to their headquarters. Then I can finally complete my mission without anyone getting in my way."

Freddy was nodding vigorously, his eyes filling with excitement.

Auntie and Scarlett stared at Maya, and Maya stared defiantly back. They were so consumed in their argument, in the waves of anger that rocked between them, that they only noticed what had happened when it was already too late.

A muffled voice cried out beside Maya, and three pairs of eyes snapped to the scene unfolding there. Maya stood agape, frozen, barely breathing, as Freddy, with large, gloved hands covering his mouth, was dragged away by two tall, cloaked figures.

"Maya!" Freddy screamed as best he could, tears beginning to stream down his face. His eyes flickered, the colors changing in an almost hesitant fashion, as though they too were afraid.

"NO!" Maya shrieked, as Freddy, his heels digging into the earth, was pulled farther and farther away.

And then she was unfrozen, and she bolted after the OCT, after Freddy.

CHAPTER 11

Followers (Again)

There was only one thought in Maya's mind as she sprinted after Freddy and his kidnappers: *Save him.*

And yet Maya was not scared—no. Her whole mind was consumed with anger, both with the fury she had released against Flora and Scarlett and the rage that she felt now at seeing Freddy taken away.

He couldn't be gone. He couldn't leave her when he had helped her so much. He had been there for her, in the short time they'd known each other, Maya thought, and it would be unjustly cruel for their friendship to be cut short.

Through the market Maya tore, whipping around corners, running into shoppers and pushing aside little kids so that she wouldn't lose Freddy. How could they take him? And yet some very small, still-rational part of Maya's brain wondered why they hadn't taken her instead. After all, she was the one trying to hunt them down.

A thought sprang into her head. If she kept following the OCT, if she didn't try to confront them—or, at least, not yet—they just might lead her to their base. Then she could finish them once and for all.

As her tunic billowed behind her and the market, with all its scents and chattering voices, grew farther behind her, Auntie's voice came unbidden into Maya's mind: *Do you know how many people are even in the OCT?*

Maya scowled and shook off the question. No, she didn't, but that didn't really matter, did it? The prophecy said that she was going to be the one to defeat the OCT, so whatever happened, she figured, the OCT would end up being beaten.

Unless it isn't your time. You're only eleven. Now it was Scarlett's voice.

"Go away!" Maya yelled, slowing down a little bit, swatting at nonexistent flies over her head.

She stopped running for a moment and looked around. The market had to be at least a hundred yards away now. A pang of sadness struck her heart. All that humanity, all that life, and she would never see it again—or at least she wouldn't ever see the same market again.

She then looked out in front of her, to the west, where the afternoon sun would soon be hitting her face. Squinting, she could make out several cloaked figures, one of them with something slung over his back. No, Maya realized, not something. Someone. Freddy. Even as Maya stood still for just a moment, they seemed to be quickly growing farther away.

She sighed, swallowed with some difficulty, wiped the sweat off her brow, and then began running again. She knew that she could run for much longer than a human, but that didn't mean she could run forever. In about two or three hours, she figured, she would need to stop and rest, preferably in a place with water.

And yet the OCT were moving faster than she. But, she thought, fueled by fury and rage, she might just be able to catch up to them.

One of the OCT had stayed behind while the others fled with Freddy. Once Maya had run off too, he drew a knife. He fought with Scarlett and Auntie, their blades flashing in the air, their muscles tight—though Auntie thought it rather seemed that their opponent was more dedicated to stalling them than actually hurting them. And indeed, after several minutes, without so much as a word, the man ran off, leaving them in the market, reeling as they thought through what had just happened.

"What are we going to do?" Scarlett asked.

"I . . ." Now that they weren't fighting anymore, Auntie was still in shock from all of the things Maya had said, and the way she had exploded in anger, a volcano proportional to Mount Vesuvius raining lava the way she exuded volatile fury. And then how Freddy was just *taken* and Maya just *left*. "I . . . guess we follow them."

"How do we know where to go, though?"

Auntie paced around for a moment, drawing several suspicious glances from passersby, which she ignored. "I actually don't think that we really need to hurry."

Scarlett stared incredulously. "But . . . but you want to find Maya."

"I do. I do." *More than you could possibly know.* Just the thought caused Auntie's heart to ache. There had to be a way for Maya to forgive them, for them to make amends, to make everything better.

"But you're forgetting," she continued, "that we have two things that neither the OCT nor Maya have."

Scarlett tilted her head

"You," Auntie said, "and the teleporter."

"But we've got nothing of Maya's for me to use my power on," Scarlett said.

"Oh . . ." Auntie looked crestfallen. "Then I guess . . ."

"Wait. You—you gave Maya your cloak when we were back in the cave. She doesn't have it anymore, of course, but even that small time . . ."

"You really think you could see Maya by using the cloak?"

Scarlett, who had now also started pacing, nodded vigorously. "Yes. Yes, I think I can. I think—I mean, I don't think I would have been able to do this a while ago, but now I've used my power more than ever and I've used it to see Maya more than ever, so I don't know. I'm used to seeing her, so . . . yes." She couldn't help laughing. "Back in the Land, I never would've imagined this happening to me."

Auntie was grinning. "I never would have imagined it either."

"So . . . what now?"

"I say we should go back to the cave. We don't want to attract any more attention here—and certainly we don't want people seeing you use your power."

Scarlett nodded, and together they weaved their way back through the market.

Auntie felt as if the world was whirling at her feet, spinning around and around, threatening to throw her off each time. This was it. They were getting close to the end, close to their last chance to save Maya. But with all her centuries of experience, she had no clue as to what would happen next.

Maya followed the OCT throughout the afternoon. She crossed what she would've thought were beautiful meadows, with long, waving grasses and delicate flowers, but now, in this moment, they were only obstacles. The grasses whipped at her legs, leaving behind faint scratches and a few trickles of blood, and the flowers were left trampled and ruined, smushed to the ground.

While the sky overhead was a soft blue dotted with pretty clouds, Maya would've preferred a grey sky, a marbled, stormy one, perhaps with rain to cool off her sweat-soaked back and face.

It was about fifty minutes after Maya's chase had led her close to a town, a cute stone place with window boxes on all of the houses, and little kids playing on tire swings, that she came upon a stream.

The stream, or rather the brook, was about a yard wide and two feet deep. It flowed quickly, however, gurgling over rocks in its path, whispering to the air with a steady *shhhhhh*. Maya knelt down on the soft grass that was its bank, cupped her hands, and drank greedily. The water was sweet and rejuvenating, as delicious as a piece of candy. It was also icy cold, and Maya splashed it on her face, relishing in the respite from the heat that it brought. She could've stayed there forever, resting, sent to sleep by the lullaby of the water, but with each moment she stopped, the OCT was growing even farther away, their black-cloaked figures becoming even smaller. All afternoon, the distance between them had hovered at around five-hundred yards, give or take. But now, when Maya's legs grew sore and she saw stars before her eyes due to tiredness, the gap was more like a thousand.

If she was being honest with herself, Maya was surprised that she still had the energy to keep going. Her anger now felt less pronounced; it had sunk into that pit in her stomach, still active, but not raging. In its place, a sense of excitement rose in her chest. Soon she would find the OCT's hideout.

She stood up, sighing. At the moment it hurt to walk, to put any weight on her legs. She was viscerally reminded of the time before the orphanage, before she had finally lost the ability to time travel, when every part of her had ached. *Time travel.* The words were a curse in her mind. What if she needed to time travel to get to wherever she was going? *Then I'll do it*, she told herself. *I'll time travel. Somehow.*

With that, she stretched and then leapt nimbly over the brook, resuming her chase.

Around sunset, the OCT entered a forest and Maya followed. Beams of orange-gold light broke through the canopy of the trees, giving the woods an enchanted feel. She crept along, unable to run for fear of tripping over a hidden root, silent so that she might determine where the OCT had gone.

She assumed they were going to spend the night here. Her eyes flitted back and forth as she peered around the trees, searching for footprints, or anything that indicated a campsite. Listening carefully, all she could hear was the faint chirp of birds, soft and melodic, or the rustle of leaves as a squirrel darted up a tree. The air was light and quiet, so peaceful.

She doubted she had ever been in a place this tranquil. And then she heard a shout, followed by a sort of laugh. *Freddy*. It echoed through the woods, and in a flash she was on its trail, sprinting lightly toward its origin. *Find Freddy*.

Within a few minutes she reached a clearing. There, standing on a bed of bright green grass, were the eight figures she had been following. One figure, the tallest one, the one whose arm was wrapped tightly around Freddy, was showing the others a piece of paper with his free hand. They all nodded at what they saw, and then the figure stuffed the paper into his robes.

"Ready?" he asked, his voice a growl.

The others murmured assent, and slowly they began to fade. Maya scowled. They were time traveling. How was she to know where, though?

And then Freddy, whose eyes had been downcast, looked up, looked into the trees, and, as he faded, saw Maya. His eyes went wide, and with a bleeding hand, he reached inside his captor's robes. A torn piece of paper fluttered to the ground, and then they were gone.

Maya stood there at the edge of the trees for a moment,

shocked into stillness. And then the spell was broken. She stepped into the clearing, her feet cracking a fallen twig in half. The sound spread through the forest, an outsider in the silence, and Maya winced. Then she moved forward to pick the paper up.

Back in the cave, Scarlett clutched Auntie's cloak and willed herself to see Maya. The scene was hazy, foggier than usual—though Scarlett supposed that was because, as she'd told Auntie, there was only a small connection between Maya and the cloak.

Maya was standing in a clearing in a dark forest. She bent down to pick up something at her feet. A piece of paper. Scarlett held her breath as she watched.

Maya held the paper carefully, as though it were fragile. As she peered at it, Scarlett looked too, over her shoulder.

June 10. The time with the yellow flag. 15 Harding.

Scarlett woke up with a gasp. Auntie was crouched next to her in the cave on the rocky ground. "What? What? What did you see?"

As soon as Scarlett had described the scene to Auntie, they stood up, slung their bags over their backs, and teleported away—toward the forest, and Maya.

Maya's mind was racing. *15 Harding. 15 Harding Street.* She had been right. She clutched her necklace. She was going back to 15 Harding Street, the place she had thought about ever since she was a little kid. Maya almost laughed with delight, almost cried. She had been right!

Then she focused. "The time with the yellow flag," she muttered to herself. What does it mean?

No time like the present to find out, another part of her

mind answered.

She took a deep breath and then closed her eyes, willing herself to the grey beach. Much to her surprise, she appeared there. The wind whipped her hair around, and the waves roared as they crashed upon the sand. It took immense effort for her to move, and she felt aches creeping up all over her arms and legs, but she was walking, making her way into the water.

Freddy. Think of Freddy. You're going to save him. You're going to find him. These thoughts sustained her as she inched into the tide. *Freddy. Freddy.* She was light-headed, but she was now at the end of the sandbar. Shivering, tired, she dove into the ocean.

She didn't remember the water ever being so turbulent. As she swam, she felt as if at any moment she might be swept away, forced off the face of the Earth. The sea seemed to rock and shake, no longer steady. Still, she swam on, the cold biting her ankles.

Finally, she blinked, and there in front of her, was the Tunnel of Time. As frigid as Maya was, its sight warmed her up. Oh, how she had missed it! A part of her heart felt restored as she swam into its depths, searching for the right scene. What did "the yellow flag" mean? What would happen if she missed it?

Doubt enveloped her, almost as strong as the water all around her. And then she saw the scene.

So far, none of them were what she was looking for. They all showed the forest—unadorned with a yellow marker—or even a field, from before the forest existed. Then she saw it: the forest scene—though it was night— with a yellow flag hanging from a tree like a banner. A surge of excitement caused her stomach to flip, and before she knew it, she was traveling through the scene. The water carried her back to the beach, which was as stormy as ever, and she willed herself to return.

Suddenly she was there in the forest. She grinned. She had time traveled! She had really done it! Voices— the OCT—echoed in the distance, and she followed them, continuing her chase into the night.

Ten minutes later, she had left the forest behind, replaced it with a road leading into a town. Far in the distance, she could see cloaked figures. A feeling of relief swept over her as she saw a figure dangling over one of their shoulders. Freddy.

Soon she came to a sign by the road. "Welcome to Shellside." Thrill filled her. She was here. She was in Shellside! And this time, she told herself, she wouldn't get hit by a bicycle. No, this time she was here to defeat the OCT, to finally fulfil the prophecy.

She sprinted along Main Street. And then she was there, turning left, staring down the street. It was empty now in the dark, except for a few people striding down the sidewalk. Streetlights lined the road, casting pools of light. She hesitantly stepped forward, waiting for someone to jump out at her, to keep her from walking to number 15. But nothing happened. No one noticed as she crossed the street with a light in her eye.

She peered into the dark display window at 15 Harding. Glass cases lined the room, all, she imagined, filled with jewelry—necklaces and earrings, rings and bracelets. She stepped back and looked at the awning over the shop. "Jewelry," it read. She could tell there had once been a word in front of "jewelry," but it was faded, illegible.

She tried to open the front door, but it was locked. She sighed. She could break in, she supposed, but then she might get caught and get in trouble with the police.

She scanned the storefront, looking for an open window, a vent, anything. And then her eyes rested on another door on the right side of the shop. It was grey, made of metal.

She rushed over to it. "Employees Only." She tried it; it swung smoothly inward and, her breath fast, she stepped into 15 Harding Street.

CHAPTER 12

15 Harding Street (Again)

Maya's heart was pounding and her head felt light. In front of her were stairs going down to what she could only assume was the OCT's base. Behind her was Harding Street, so peaceful, so oblivious to the danger she faced. Half of her wanted to turn on her heel, to run away and never come back to this place—she could return to warm June air and cheerful, bustling human life instead of following these stone stairs into a damp, humid basement. But she didn't. She had come this far; there was no turning back now. Besides, she told herself, Freddy was down there. Freddy, and the answers to her questions. And her parents. And her destiny, her fate. Weights upon weights were being stacked on her shoulders, so many that she felt she might crumple to the floor. What if her parents were alive? But what if they didn't remember her? Or if they were dead . . .

Again she wanted to flee. She fingered her necklace, shivering in fear. Swallowing, she made up her mind. She would go down the stairs, and she would face the OCT. She had fought them before, she remembered, and she could do it again. Besides, this time, she thought, patting its sheath, she had her dagger. She pushed the door closed. She expected it to slam, to echo and announce her presence. But it was silent, which somehow was more eerie.

She lifted her pack and placed a foot forward. And then another. And then another. As she descended the stairs, her footsteps made no sound. The staircase wound deeper and deeper into the Earth; the air was humid, dank.

Her shoulders were tensed even more than usual, and she kept glancing from side to side, expecting someone—or something—to jump out and attack her. However, her confidence grew with each passing step. *I can do this, I can do this*, she thought vigorously. And by the time she could see a light at the bottom of the stairs, she believed it.

Her hand on the hilt of her dagger, she stepped into the light, blinking a few times, disoriented, as she adjusted to the well-lit room. She was a plank of wood, stiff and immovable.

Around the room were tables, maps, scattered weapons with their blades gleaming brightly in the harsh LED lighting. Doors upon doors led out of this room: she counted at least fifteen in the concrete walls. She suddenly recalled the mysterious doors in the police station in London. She shivered, swallowed nervously, and turned to look at the center of the room.

Overall, she thought, it looked like a permanent settlement. The only thing missing was the people. And then she heard it—a scuffle from behind one of the doors on the left wall. Voices were mumbling, a chair scraping the concrete floor. One voice sounded particularly familiar. Forgetting all caution, she launched herself into the room and toward the door labeled "Orange."

"Freddy?!"

No one answered. All was still, like a stagnant pool of water growing filthy with scum.

And then the "Orange" door burst open. Five cloaked figures emerged, tall and threatening, their faces shadowed. She would've jumped backward out of their way, but she was tired of feeling weak. Now she would be strong. She would complete the prophecy.

Behind the figures, she saw Freddy tied to a chair. "Freddy," Maya breathed, her eyes shining nervously. He looked into her eyes, and she saw determination, even pleasure, etched into his slightly bruised face. She thought. *What had he always said? "I always knew I was destined for something great."*

She tried to absorb that mentality and stood up straighter. "Let him go," she growled, and she was surprised to find that her voice didn't shake.

"No," said a figure on Freddy's left, the tallest of them all. He spoke as if he were reprimanding a small child.

"I said *let him go!*" Maya's voice was growing louder, anger bubbling in her stomach.

"And I said no." His voice was calm, which only served to aggravate her further.

"Do you know who I am?" Maya was on her tippy-toes now, trying fruitlessly to match the height of the cloaked figure. Her palm clenched the hilt of her dagger dangerously, her knuckles white.

"Ye—

"I am the one—the one in the prophecy! The one who will defeat you and end you!"

"I know," the figure said, and as he spoke, he pulled his hood down. She had expected him to be grotesque, to look evil. This was not the case. Instead, chiseled features made up an alarmingly handsome face. And alarming was the right word. For though his dark brown hair was swept in just the right direction, and though his eyes were a poignant grey, there was something off about him. The lines of his face were drawn like daggers, and his hair could've been a strong wind, ready to blow the world off its feet, while his eyes could've been a storm brewing at sea. And his voice, too, was unusual. So melodic, so beautiful, but also strangely off-putting, as if it was too melodic, too beautiful. "And," he added, "do you know who I am?"

"No," Maya spat out, recovering from her shock, "and

I don't care. Release my friend *right now*." She drew her dagger and pointed it at the man.

"Tsk, tsk. They really don't teach you children anything up in the Land anymore. And Maya," he chided, as she flinched slightly at the sound of her name, "do you know how foolish you've been? To place your trust in a mere human?"

Maya was too angry to be overly rankled by this comment. "He is my friend. Let him go!"

The man held his arms out in a helpless gesture. "Sorry. No can do. But it's so cute how you think he's your friend. I mean, he's just a human." The other figures laughed. "How do you know he'd hold up under torture?"

This offhand remark did penetrate Maya's armor of rage. She stumbled slightly. "You—you—"

"You know, it is a shame to confide in someone whose skin can break at the slightest touch . . ." The man said, a grin spreading across his face, and before Maya knew what was happening, a knife was being held to Freddy's neck.

Fear seeped through her armor. "No, no, please," she said breathlessly, unable to look away from Freddy's face, his eyes watering with tears.

"I'll let him go now, if you want," the man said amicably. "I'll release his soul from these chains." The knife pressed further into Freddy's neck, and a bead of blood ran down his skin.

"No. No." Maya was desperately trying to hold her tears back, trying to regain her confidence. It flickered in and out, a sort of mirage. "Don't do it." Now her voice was strong and sharp.

"Sorry." The man shrugged, and the knife slipped into Freddy's neck. Maya stared at the blood spouting from her friend, and she stumbled, falling back against a table. Her eyes seemed glued to the scene, forced to watch as more blood spilled, gushing like a waterfall, and the light in Freddy's perpetually changing eyes went out.

"No, no, no, no!" Maya could hardly see anything through her tears, but she still held her knife out in front in case anyone tried to stab her too. Freddy. He was gone. Just like that. Her mind raced, back to when they'd first met, to how they'd become friends, how they'd planned to take on the OCT all by themselves. How could he be dead? There had been so much life left in him; he had talked on and on about all of the things he would do with his life. And now ...

Something stirred in her blurred vision. And it looked like it was coming from ... Freddy? With her free hand, she wiped her tears away, sniffling slightly. Yes, it was Freddy. He was blinking, and the man was cutting his binds. Someone else was handing him a napkin to wipe off the blood. He stood up and stretched. Maya looked on in utter bewilderment, completely sure she was dreaming. She pinched herself. No, it wasn't a dream. But then ... what was it?

"Blood is such a nuisance," Freddy was saying. "Wright, look at my neck, will you?"

The tall man bent down to look at the place where the knife had slit Freddy's throat. "It's already closing up, my lord."

My lord? Maya coughed, and all eyes flicked to her. Had they tricked her with Freddy's death? Had Freddy been tricking her this whole time?

"What is going on?" she asked, her anger rising up again.

"Ah," Wright said simply. "I forgot. Our young guest was not in on the plan. My lord, if you could assume your normal form."

Normal form? Maya's brow furrowed, confusion mixing with anger.

She watched as Freddy, the eleven-year-old boy she'd met at the orphanage, melted, dissolving into a puddle on the floor. She cried out, but Wright held a finger up. "Wait."

The puddle was now reforming itself, somewhat like an ice sculpture melting in reverse, until a grown man stood where Freddy had been. He was dressed in black robes, and Maya figured that if fake-Freddy turned around, an octagon would be emblazoned on the back.

"Who are you?" Maya asked incredulously, anger surging up again. The man had the same face as Freddy, the same hair, same freckles, and same eyes. But there was a sneer on his features, a sneer that Freddy never would've had.

"You two already know each other, I think," Wright said silkily. "Or, at least, m'lord knows you."

"Yes. Hello, Maya. Allow me to introduce myself properly. My name is Fredrick von Hopsburg."

Maya was shell shocked. *Fredrick von Hopsburg. Freddy von Hopsburg. Freddy.* "It—it was you the whole time? You knew our plan from the very beginning?" Maya was shaking.

"Of course I did. I was waiting at the orphanage for you to show up. Just a bit of old magic to make everyone think I'd been living there for a while. After all, it was I who arranged for you to end up in London." He smiled a horrible smile. "You showed up, as I thought you would, with absolutely no self-esteem. You were lost. And I was there to make sure you were found."

"Everything you said to me. Our whole friendship . . ."

"A lie. I knew you'd be drawn to someone with a strong sense of direction. And so I made sure I was that person. It was so, so simple.

"And, Maya, as I got to know you, I found you to be such a stubborn character. A quality I admire very much. I was desperately disappointed that I would have to kill you in the end. You are the one in the prophecy, after all, and I did mean to end you along with your parents that day that we"—he gestured to his companions—"showed up at your house."

"My parents," Maya said quietly, her voice barely audible. She clutched her necklace tightly, tighter than ever before. "They're dead?"

"Oh, yes. Of course they are. We killed them five years ago to this particular Earth-day, I think . . . You didn't sincerely believe that they would be alive, did you?"

Before Maya could answer, he continued:

"And, you know, that was a thing about you that I found rather strange. For as smart as you were, you were so gullible. You never once suspected that Freddy wasn't who he claimed to be."

"Don't say his name," Maya hissed.

"Oh, child. You can't mourn those who were never real in the first place."

His words stung Maya, and she longed to retort, but von Hopsburg had started speaking again.

"Your friend—Scarlett, I believe? Now, she knew something was off with me from the very start. Smart one, she is. You know," he added, "we've been keeping tabs on you, your aunt, and Scarlett since you all came to Earth. And that friend of yours is quite impressive. Uses her powers very well. Especially for someone at such a young age. Remarkable."

Maya was shaking even more severely, as though she was a fire of burning rage, and every mention of Freddy, of her parents—was it true, they were dead?—of Scarlett was gasoline being poured on. There was only so much more she could take.

"Well," von Hopsburg said—and Maya cringed at the

fact that he sounded exactly like Freddy—"That's my story. And it was foolish of you to come here, Maya. Because we're going to kill you."

"No. You're not." Maya spoke the words as if she was a small child.

"Yes, we are."

But their argument didn't get any further, because suddenly two people appeared at the bottom of the stairs, daggers out. Auntie and Scarlett.

This was too much for Maya. She started to lunge at Wright—she couldn't attack von Hopsburg, not now, when he reminded her so much of Freddy—but Auntie was beside her in a flash, holding her back.

"Flora. What are you doing here?" Maya growled as she tried to break free.

"We're going to help you," Scarlett said, appearing beside Auntie.

"I don't want help."

"Well, we're giving it to you anyway," Auntie told her.

"Let me go!" Maya yelled.

"No! I won't let you!"

"You can't tell me what to do." Maya's voice was bitter and mean. "Freddy's gone—he never was real—and my parents are dead. Dead! This is my battle, not yours!"

"But Maya—"

Maya had broken free of her grasp, and Auntie and Scarlett watched in horror as she lunged at Wright. Then they looked at each other and plunged into battle after her.

CHAPTER 13

The Prophecy

Maya didn't even really know how to fight with a dagger; she'd never been taught in the Land. So she used a combination of jabs and swipes to attack anything that came near her and let her fist do most of the talking. In all honesty, she realized, she didn't know how to fight with her fists either, but that was of less concern. All she had to do was try to sink her knuckles into Wright's perfect face, or chest, or anywhere else.

They moved back and forth, back and forth, locked in their deadly dance. Perhaps Wright was going easy on her, letting her live so that von Hopsburg could kill her, but there was no doubt that Maya's agility and speed made her a dangerous opponent, whether she knew what she was doing or not.

Out of the corner of her eye, Maya saw that Auntie and Scarlett had taken on the other four Octagons, while von Hopsburg stood off to the side, watching the battle unfold. Scarlett and Auntie did make a good team, and after such a long time of being together, they were quite attuned to each other's instincts and were able to fight in a graceful, elegant manner, bobbing and weaving through their opponents like needles through a tapestry.

Maya herself parried and ducked, rage burning in her eyes. Wright seemed vaguely amused by their fight at first, but as Maya's intensity grew, as she scored her first hit, slicing her blade across the top of his knuckles, his eyes hardened.

"Why don't you go play with von Hopsburg?" he

taunted her, leaning back to avoid a punch. "Or does he look too much like your dear friend Freddy?"

Maya was boiling over with anger. It wasn't so much that what Wright had said was true, but that he had had the nerve to say it. She growled. The corners of her eyes stung. *Don't cry. Don't cry.* She charged again at Wright.

"Come on, little girl." His voice was bubbling with menace. "If you are the one in the prophecy, you ought to defeat the leader of the OCT. Also, aren't you supposed to have powers?"

Maya's breath was shaky. She herself had been thinking about that for the past several minutes. The prophecy did say she was supposed to have "impressive powers." So where were they? Were they just waiting until the last moment to unveil themselves?

Her chest heaved up and down as she caught her breath for a moment, recalibrating her mind. *Must fight. Must fight.* Deep inside her brain, though, something that was locked up wanted to be freed. *Freddy. He's gone. He's gone. Don't we have the right to cry? Your parents. They're gone. They're gone. Don't we have the right to cry?*

I do. I do. I do have the right to cry. Maya's face was softening. *But I can't. I have to fight. I have to fight?* Confusion was overtaking her. It was all too much, the prophecy, the fight. Couldn't she just lay her weapon down, just let everything subside? Wasn't she allowed to grieve?

Just then, von Hopsburg appeared by Wright's side. When Maya refocused, she saw not one but two opponents. Even so, in her confused state of mind she couldn't really tell the difference. To take down two was better than one, she told herself, and so she advanced.

Everything faded from her mind: the background sounds of Auntie and Scarlett fighting, the stench of sweat. She blinked, suddenly aware of her breathing, of her heartbeat. And then von Hopsburg lunged at her.

Maya was locked in the fight. She could think of nothing except hurting Wright and von Hopsburg for . . . something she couldn't even remember at the moment. All thoughts about 15 Harding Street, about the prophecy, about Freddy, were gone. The only thing that mattered was the fight.

She used her dagger in her right hand to fight Wright, and her left fist to fight von Hopsburg. Still, they were forcing her to retreat, and she knew that with a few more steps, she would be up against a wall.

She parried a thrust from Wright and curved her arm to knock aside von Hopsburg's as his knife advanced also. The weight of her punch threw his aim off, and she punched again, right in his shoulder.

Then Auntie and Scarlett appeared by Maya's side. She scowled when she saw them. "I don't want your help." She shoved Auntie off to the side, receiving a punch to her shoulder from Wright.

"I don't care whether you want it or not."

Maya's anger was mixing with a deep-seated confusion, and the two did not go well together. She felt as though she had a bomb inside her, just waiting to explode, as Wright and von Hopsburg finally penned her in.

She was breathing fast. Was this the end? Would she die by von Hopsburg's hand, by Freddy's hand? Auntie watched on, her mouth helplessly open, as Scarlett continued to fight. Scarlett was tattooed with bruises, Maya saw, but that didn't worry her. Bruises weren't serious injuries.

Maya was staring at Wright and von Hopsburg. Von Hopsburg grinned an evil grin. "Guess you're not the one in the prophecy after all. Too bad." He raised his knife, and it was then that Maya saw it: Von Hopsburg's legs were spread apart in a fighting stance—only a small child could slide between them. Falling to the floor, Maya darted through his legs and emerged standing on the other side, just as his knife clanged against the wall.

Auntie rushed over to Maya.

"Don't want your help . . ."

"But Maya—"

"I said, *I don't want it!* I never have! Let me fight my own fight." Her words were laced with poison, and her vision seemed to be tinted with red, as a combination of anger and fear and confusion and a million other things crashed over her, a monstrous wave in a hurricane. Perhaps she was the hurricane, and it was collapsing in on itself. "Why don't you stop getting in the way of my destiny? Don't you want me to live up to my potential? I mean, you've always believed in me, right? Or were you just saying that?" Maya stalked away, tensing her shoulders as she did so.

The sound of knife upon knife rang out from Scarlett's general direction. Maya took no notice, and, ignoring her aching arms and a small cut that pulsed blood on her thigh, prepared to fight again.

She was growing tired, moving more sluggishly. And yet the intensity fighting required seemed to temporarily abate the bomb inside her, to slow the countdown for a little while. And so Maya took pleasure in fighting, in trying to harm the people who had done so much to harm her, and she was glad to see she was having an effect on them.

Wright had now taken off his robe entirely, revealing a black tunic, and Freddy—no, it was von Hopsburg—was shedding his as well.

Her fight with Wright and von Hopsburg had twisted and turned so that Maya was now standing on top of a table while Wright and von Hopsburg taunted her and smirked, their weapons down for the moment.

"Why don't you come and join us, little Maya? We

would be glad to have you on our side."

"It's too bad you're going to die eventually. You've put up a fight, though."

"Are you afraid to hurt me because I look like your friend?"

"We can teach you things you'd have never learned otherwise."

"We're not the bad guys."

"We're not the bad guys."

Their words were vipers circling Maya, threatening to sink their teeth into her, threatening to be believable. Because there was some irrational part of Maya that wanted to trust them.

"Or will you die like your parents?" one of them was saying.

That question jolted Maya back to reality. As upset, as distraught as she was, she could never forget her parents, never forget that they had been killed by the OCT, the people who were trying to kill her now. Amidst all the confusion, that was one thing that was as clear as the day, the eye of the hurricane.

"Never," she whispered. "I'll never join you."

Her opponents shrugged, and in the few seconds as they raised their daggers to fight once more, Maya took advantage of this to look out over the room. First, she saw Scarlett, pinned down by three of the OCT. Blood streamed from her nose, and there were small gashes on both of her cheeks. Her enemies were binding her, forcing her to kneel on the cold, hard ground. Maya's face flickered with sadness.

Then she saw Auntie. One of the OCT had bound her arms and legs, though from what Maya could see, there was no need, as Auntie was either unconscious—or worse. Auntie's face was battered with blood and bruises, and a large cut spilled blood down her leg. Terror shot through

Maya, and she called out: "No!"

The Octagon was dragging Auntie away through one of the mysterious doors on the side of the room, the ones that reminded Maya so strongly of that decrepit police station in London.

"No!" she cried again, and felt like she was spinning, falling off the Earth. She had pushed Auntie away and ignored her, and now . . . *It's all my fault.*

She stood on the edge of the table—though it felt more like a cliff—helpless and alone. Freddy—no, von Hopsburg; why was it so hard to remember?—and Wright grinned terribly at her. "See? Everything is lost, little girl."

"I'm not little."

"You're only eleven," Wright hissed, and his voice didn't sound melodic anymore.

You're only eleven. Scarlett had said the same thing. Maya looked over to where her friend—but was Scarlett still her friend?—was captive. Scarlett would barely meet her eye.

"No. No." The hurricane was growing stronger inside her. She was splattered with its water. She could feel its winds tearing at her skin. Soon, so soon, it would carry her away, or the bomb would go off, or something else terrible would happen.

Her mind was racing, sprinting, to the point where any runner would've been bent over, sick. *Only eleven . . . parents . . . Freddy . . . dead . . . Auntie . . .*

Fear, anger, guilt, confusion. Fear, anger, guilt, confusion. Fear anger guilt confusion. Fearangerguiltconfusion. fearangerguiltconfusion.

Tick, tick, tick.

Winds roaring.

Voices hissing. Maya couldn't tell whether they were real or not; she thought she could make out von

Hopsburg, Wright, Scarlett all mouthing things, but she couldn't hear them.

She was melting.

Falling through the ground.

Falling through the Earth.

Falling,

Falling.

Until she fell no more.

A fire, blazing all around her. And yet it didn't burn her skin. It was warm, comforting. Visions swirled before her eyes.

The necklace.

You'll know how to find us.

Heat rising.

Maya rising.

Rising through the Earth.

Rising through the ground.

Tick-tick-tick.

Rising—

Tick-tick-tick.

Rising—

Tick-

tick-

tick—

Light exploded out of Maya.

It seemed like she was floating, and a halo of light, which had wreathed her body, had burst across the room.

She felt her mouth open in a scream but could not distinguish her own cries from the others', others who she could not see. The necklace on her chest burned hot against her skin.

And then it was over. She fell limp, crashing down onto the table. Maps and papers flew everywhere. Everything went black.

CHAPTER 14

The Return

Maya opened her eyes and blinked blearily. Everything around her was blurry, just smudges against a grey background. She heard footsteps approach and sat up, reaching for her dagger. Squinting, she saw Scarlett's platinum blonde hair. She released her grip.

"Are you okay?" Scarlett asked. In addition to the blood on her face, Scarlett now had a purple lump on her forehead. Maya stared dazedly at it. Where had it come from?

"Yeah, yeah. I think," she answered slowly, stretching her arms out and examining herself. There were no gashes on her body—at least, not that she could see. In fact, on the whole, she seemed to be radiating a warm glow.

She hopped off the table and looked around the room. Auntie lay face down on the ground, and chairs and tables were flipped over and strewn everywhere, while the lights on the ceiling swayed and flickered. No one else was there, though. Von Hopsburg, Wright, all the rest—gone.

"What happened?"

Scarlett bit her lip. "I'm not entirely sure."

They spoke to one another as if they were two volatile substances that could only be mixed under extreme caution.

"You—you kind of went rigid," she continued, choosing her words carefully. "You know, like a piece of wood. And then you were floating, and this light . . . it seemed to come from out of your necklace, and then it covered you." She paused and swallowed.

"What then?" Maya asked tentatively.

"Well, then it kind of exploded. Like one of those human bombs. And it shook the whole room." She gestured around, and it was then that Maya noticed little cracks in the wall, the kind that emerge after an earthquake.

"It, um, it . . . there was a, like, a rope of light, and it kind of flashed out and hit the—the one that, um, looked like Freddy . . ." She muttered the last part, as if unsure whether Maya would lash out at her. "And then it spread. It went from one Octagon to the next, and there were a bunch of light-ropes that went through the walls and the ceiling. And . . . and then they were all gone, and you fell. There was another aftershock or something, and I hit my head. That's about it."

Maya nodded. She took a deep breath and looked down at her chest. Her necklace was glowing, glowing more than she herself was. It seemed to be like a little sun blazing with light. All of a sudden, she felt faint. She looked around again and saw Auntie. The situation registered this time. She almost fell over with shock at the sight of her covered in bruises and cuts.

Scarlett caught Maya before she tipped over. "Here. Sit down."

Sitting on the floor now, Maya pointed mutely at Auntie and mouthed the words that she couldn't say. "Will she be okay?"

Scarlett sighed. "I don't know."

Maya nodded, tears filling her eyes. How many times had she put other people in danger because of her own selfishness? How many times had she been reckless and stupid and not bothered with what other people told her? She had trusted Freddy, for crying out loud! She, the one in the prophecy, had believed everything he'd told her. And she had been the one in the prophecy—she had just proved that.

She began to cry now, but quietly. She didn't deserve to be the one, not after everything that had happened with Auntie, with everything. How could she have been so stupid when her parents died to save her? What was she thinking? Maya tucked her knees to her chest and thought that she might never move again.

After some time, Scarlett shook her shoulder. "We should go. Auntie isn't doing well."

Maya looked up.

"She's alive, but . . ." Scarlett said.

Maya's stomach twisted. It was the worst feeling she had ever felt.

Scarlett took a deep breath. "We need to go back to the Land."

Maya flinched.

"Maya, you're a hero now," Scarlett reminded her, with only a hint of resentment in her tired voice. "You won't be in trouble."

Maya thought about this. "How do we get up there?" Her voice was raspy.

"I-I—" Scarlett stuttered. "My mom . . . when she comes down to Earth, to get back up, she . . . I don't—I don't know." Scarlett hesitated. "Um," she began, "your parents . . . we could try just yelling? Maybe that'll work?"

Maya had only half been listening to what Scarlett said. It wasn't that she'd been thinking some deep thoughts, more that she hadn't been. She'd just been staring off into space, feeling shell shocked, like a soldier who was just returning from war. "Yeah, sure," she said absently to Scarlett.

Scarlett looked relieved. "All right. Let's go."

Scarlett helped Maya to her feet and then the two of them awkwardly draped Auntie's arms around their shoulders so they could carry her along. Maya felt numb as they dragged themselves up the steps away from the OCT headquarters, from the scene of the fight.

After struggling up the stairs for a few minutes, the two of them reached the exit onto Harding Street. Scarlett heaved the door open and stepped out into . . . sunlight. It had been dark when they'd descended.

They both blinked distractedly as they stood on the sidewalk. "I guess we were both unconscious for a while," Scarlett said.

Maya nodded. She was surprised too. But the sunlight was welcoming and warm and felt soothing. She looked up and down the street. Shoppers and passersby were striding up and down the sidewalks, and the shops were open, their windows shining, their awnings bright and cheerful. A sea breeze wafted through the street.

Maya had figured being in shock meant that she wouldn't notice her surroundings, wouldn't be paying attention to the world. And she hadn't while they were in the basement of 15 Harding Street. But now, on the street, everything stood out to her just as vividly as it had before.

The life in the air was rejuvenating, and she longed to go into the shops, longed to poke around and browse, to hear the little bell tingle as she entered a shop. Why did she feel this way? Auntie was hurt, she herself was tired and worried and mourning over Freddy, even though he hadn't even been real. She tried, with all her might, to rekindle the animosity she had felt back in the big city when she was all on her own, when she had decided that Earth was a bad place.

Even then, though, she hadn't believed that entirely, and she believed it even less so now. Earth wasn't bad; bad things happened on it, maybe, but it itself was a paradise to her. *No*, she reprimanded herself. *No, it can't be. I've done too many bad things, made too many bad decisions here to like it. I can't. I'm not supposed to.*

All these thoughts swirled around in her head as she and Scarlett made their way up toward Main Street, ignoring the strange looks they were attracting- two girls carrying an old woman.

Maya wanted to turn around, to run back down Harding Street. She wanted to laugh in the June air, to go into the bakery at the end of the street and smell the fresh bread. They turned the corner and continued down Main Street, but Maya wanted to stop, to wait at the corner for a bus to come, so that she could sit on its patterned seats and be surrounded by people and their energy.

And most of all, she thought, as they wound their way through some strangely clean alleyways, slowly leaving the town behind as they climbed the cobbled roads toward fresh green hills, she wanted to see 15 Harding Street. She had been in the basement, she realized, but never in the actual building.

And then she noticed that the sense of longing she always had felt lighter, smaller than it had been before the fight with the OCT. It was still there, but . . . she couldn't really put her finger on it, but it was strange not to feel arrogant, not to have her shoulders and neck all tightened up as she walked along on Earth.

She and Scarlett had not talked at all as they walked. There was no need for communication.

Now, though, they were standing on top of a small green hill. They'd been walking for some thirty minutes, Maya supposed, and the sun was high in the sky. In front of them, a little ways off, the sea crashed upon rocks, the water reflecting the sunlight in a delicate way, as though it were made of glass.

Scarlett coughed, and Maya turned to look at her. "This'll be the place."

Maya nodded.

Scarlett started yelling, started asking for someone to come and fetch them, and after a minute, Maya joined in. She wasn't sure how she felt about returning to the Land. It would be comforting to go back home, to the place she'd lived for basically her entire life, the place she knew by heart, and yet . . . she stopped shouting, lost in thought, until Scarlett nudged her. "Look."

A tunnel, a vacuum, was descending out of the sky, growing closer and closer.

Maya cringed as it swept them up, as vines seemed to wrap around her chest, growing tighter and tighter. She shuddered with déjà vu, thinking of the other time that she had been carried up to the Land of the Clouds. She had hoped to never travel this way again, but oh well.

Finally, they emerged. They were inside the Chamber of the Transport, the building where the tunnels were housed, where Scarlett and Auntie had departed, though Maya didn't know that.

They stood in awkward silence, waiting for someone to find them. Then Scarlett spoke. "I guess no one's coming."

"Guess not."

"We should get to the hospital, though."

"Yep."

"We'll probably run into some official before we leave the building. They can help us carry Auntie."

"Yep."

Scarlett sighed. "I'm probably going to be in so much trouble. I mean, you defeated the OCT. And Auntie had permission to go to Earth. Me, though . . ."

"Yep."

They stood for a minute and then walked out of the chamber, wending their way back to the lobby, each thinking their own thoughts. In the lobby, the receptionist stopped them.

"Just hold on a minute," she called out to them, surveying them suspiciously. "Who are you?"

They marched over to reception with weary expressions on their faces. The receptionist scrutinized them through her thick glasses.

Maya couldn't help but see them through her eyes: two girls, not more than eleven, carrying an old lady, one wearing a glowing necklace around her neck and looking thoroughly exhausted, while the other had large amounts of dried blood on her face. All three of them were dusty, their arms and legs smudged with dirt.

"Who are you?" the receptionist repeated, her tone more curious now.

"Scarlett Clayden."

"Maya Wood."

"Wait, wait, wait," the receptionist said. "Maya, as in the one who disappeared to Earth?"

Maya grimaced at this phrasing and nodded. Didn't this lady have any idea what she'd gone through? She deserved a better title than, "the one who disappeared to Earth."

"And Scarlett. The one who disappeared a day later?"

Scarlett's grimace was bigger.

"But wasn't there one more of you? One who was actually permitted to go to Earth?"

Scarlett nodded toward Auntie's limp figure.

"Oh my god!" the receptionist cried, fully taking in the group in front of her. "Is she okay?"

Maya was quite irritated by now. "She's dying, we think. So if you could help us to a hospital . . ."

"Of—of course. Yes, I can. Follow me."

She stood up and walked, as fast as her heels would allow, over to the front door. "Rich?" she asked the security guard outside. "Would you please escort these girls to a hospital? Their companion is badly injured, and they could use a checkup as well."

"Come on, girls. You can sit on the back of my bike."

Maya had never realized how similar to cars some of the bikes in the Land were. Rich's, for instance, had a driver's seat that was like that of a normal bike, only it was partly powered by magic, so he could have a tent-like structure attached to the back where people could sit, and he could still bike fast.

Maya and Scarlett piled themselves into the back of the bike, with Auntie stretched out between them. "We'll be at the hospital in just a few minutes," Rich told them. Then he hopped on and they all rode off.

It was so strange to be back, Maya thought. Everything looked exactly the same, as if no time had passed—in fact, barely any time *had* passed—only half a day since Auntie and Scarlett had left and a day and a half for Maya—and yet so much had changed.

They rode through the city center, passing the fountain with the prophecy etched on it. Maya knew that she and Scarlett were thinking the same thing as they stared at it. Only a few days ago they had stood there, and Maya had decided she was the one in the prophecy . . . They looked sheepishly at each other.

Now they were out of the city center, near where Maya and Scarlett's houses were, in the suburbs almost. Maya knew every inch of this part of the cloud. It was surreal to be back there. Especially, she thought, when she remembered that there had been a moment—several moments, in fact—when it seemed like she might never return.

They passed a small house with a sloped roof and a tree just beside it. Maya almost laughed. How many times had she and the other neighborhood kids sat on the front lawn and watched Tzvi, the cat belonging to the couple who lived there, climb up the tree and then jump onto the roof? She supposed he was up there right now. She craned her neck to try and see, but they were moving too fast.

So many memories hit her as they approached the hospital. They were refreshing and familiar, like a cool pool in the summer, and yet she felt uncomfortable, as though she had outgrown the pool. Was it possible to outgrow your home?

The Land seemed so clean, so quiet, so colorless compared to Earth.

Just then they arrived at the hospital, and Maya's mind was drawn to more immediate matters. Auntie. Her body flooded with worry. Would the doctors be able to help her? What had even happened to her? And it was all Maya's fault . . .

CHAPTER 15

The End

Maya was curled up in a plush chair in a hallway at the hospital. Across from her, on the stark white wall, a clock. Tick-tick-tick.

She squirmed restlessly, tired but unable to sleep. Auntie was in surgery right now, in an operating room just down the hall. She had been under for about six hours. No doctor had yet come out to say whether everything would be okay.

To add to that, there seemed to be cords wrapped tight around Maya's chest. She knew exactly what they were from: her inability to time travel in the Land. She'd never noticed them before, but of course she hadn't ever time traveled before going to Earth. She hadn't been exposed to the freedom she felt when the world, when all of time, was at her fingertips.

And then there was the clock, ticking, ticking, ticking. It was driving her crazy—she wanted to lunge out of her chair and knock it off the wall, for it was so like the ticking she had felt within herself down beneath 15 Harding Street.

She closed her eyes and again tried to sleep; she couldn't remember the last time she'd had a long rest. But whenever her eyelids shut, a vision appeared in them, a vision that would not go away. *Freddy.* His face was there, smiling and waving. It wasn't von Hopsburg—no, this was Freddy. The boy who had been her friend.

Tears dripped down her face, and now the voice of von Hopsburg echoed in her ears: *You can't mourn someone who was never real.* Maybe that was true. But Freddy had been real to her, and she missed him. She really missed him.

Just then, she was aware of someone coughing. She opened her eyes to see a doctor, still in his surgery gown, standing next to her chair.

She opened her mouth to speak, but no words would come out. *Please say she's okay. Please, please.*

"She made it through the surgery," the doctor said. "She has a few sprains, a few breaks, and a terrible concussion, but did what we could."

"So, she'll be okay?" Maya whispered.

The doctor grimaced. "Well . . . she pulled through the surgery, but she still has to recover. Right now she's in a coma. We hope she wakes up."

"What?" Maya said softly, feeling dizzy. Again, guilt swept over her, threatening to throttle her. "She's . . ."

The doctor patted Maya's shoulder awkwardly. "We're moving her to a room. I'll have someone show you where it is, and you can sit with her."

Maya nodded and the doctor left.

Little did she know that rumors of her trip down to Earth were already spreading through the hospital, that the doctor was buzzing with excitement at having talked to the famous Maya, the one, they said, who had gone to Earth to complete the prophecy. Maya couldn't have cared less about what people thought, though, even if she had known. All she wanted to do was go home, to get out of this pristine, mechanical hospital. There was no life here. She envied Scarlett a bit, for she had gone home to be reunited with her parents and siblings, saying to Maya that she would come back later to check on how Auntie was doing. If only Maya could just go home to Auntie . . .

A few minutes later, a nurse came to fetch Maya and show her to Auntie's room. She was a very polite person, small in stature like Maya, with tawny hair pulled back in a bun. She left after settling Maya down in an armchair in Auntie's room, saying she would be returning soon to check on Auntie's vitals.

And so Maya sat in the small hospital room, curled up in her armchair, which was less comfortable than her seat in the hallway. Auntie lay still on the bed, covered in a thin layer of blankets, surrounded by blinking machines, tubes sticking in and out of her body. It was a pitiful sight, and Maya wanted so badly to look away, but she couldn't. She needed Auntie's presence, needed it to steady her right now, like North on a compass. And North was missing right now. North was missing.

The walls of the room were a pale blue, the color of the sky, delicate and beautiful, and a few flowers adorned them, cartoonishly painted with vibrant reds, oranges, yellows, greens, pinks, and purples. There was also a window in the room, and out of it, Maya could see most of Cloud 7 from their sixth-story perch. Maya looked up at the sky, and for a moment was astonished by what she saw—no clouds in the sky. There was nothing but blue, and the shining spot where the sun was.

Of course there weren't, Maya told herself. They lived on top of the clouds. But she was finding that perhaps she missed clouds, missed the way they hung over the world like little cotton balls, or the way that they could grow so large and threatening, a dark grey herald of oncoming storms. There would be no rain up here either, no sweet droplets of water tumbling from the sky. How had she never noticed the lack of these things before? How had she never known how much she was missing?

Eventually, she fell into a light sleep. She expected it to be free of dreams, to feel refreshing, but when she awoke only thirty minutes later, she found that there were even more things nagging at her, as if she'd dreamed something she didn't remember, something that had riled her up, gotten on her nerves.

She stood up. She couldn't sit any longer; she needed to move. Pacing around the room, she let everything that was nagging her invade her mind. She never had learned why 15 Harding Street was so important. It was the OCT stronghold, yes, but why did her necklace have the address engraved on it? And what had happened with her necklace when she summoned all of the light? What type of power was that, even?

Thirst began to scratch at her throat, and she picked up a water bottle on a small side table that she assumed had been left for her. As she drank thirstily, she heard a soft knock at the door. Scarlett was standing there in a fresh, clean tunic, her hair braided neatly.

Maya ushered her in. A silence fell between them as Maya returned to her armchair in the corner and Scarlett sat down in a plastic chair by the door. They didn't talk for several minutes. What could they say? Some link in their friendship had broken, leaving them estranged.

"That was some fight," Scarlett said, breaking the silence. "I didn't ever think I'd be fighting the OCT when I was eleven."

Maya gave a small, quiet laugh. "Yeah. It was."

Silence. It was as if Scarlett were a bear Maya was afraid to accidentally poke—and vice versa.

"Although, I mean, you didn't really need Auntie or me," Scarlett said.

"That's not ... I don't think I could've done without you."

"But how did we help? It was you—you and Freddy— who really made things happen."

Maya scoffed, though there was a twinge of sadness mixed in. "Right, Freddy."

"What, um, what ever happened to him?" Scarlett

asked. "I don't think I ever found out."

"Oh, he . . . he was von Hopsburg. Always had been." It was hard for Maya to admit.

"Ah. Oh. So it was like Sir Galiston told us—about how von Hopsburg would disguise himself as a boy."

Maya nodded. "If you and Auntie hadn't been there, though," Maya said, as much as it pained her, "I could have died. Freddy—or von Hopsburg, or whoever—could've killed me." It felt like Freddy was dying all over again because Maya was losing him, recognizing that there never had been a Freddy, that von Hopsburg had been behind everything. "Also, you and Auntie took on most of the Octagons in that fight. Thank you." It was nearly impossible for Maya to get the last two words out. The next thing she needed to do was apologize for how she'd treated Scarlett, but she wasn't ready for that yet. Maybe someday, though, she would be.

"You're welcome," Scarlett said hesitantly.

And then the question that Maya had been thinking of nonstop rose to the tip of her tongue, and she spit it out. "I just don't understand. I don't get why 15 Harding Street is on my necklace, and why my necklace started glowing in the first place." She had no clue why she was saying these things to Scarlett, but she was.

"I don't know," Scarlett mused. She paused, unsure of whether to say the next words on her mind. She took a deep breath. "I could probably help you find out, though."

Maya stared at her in amazement. "You could—"

"—use my powers to see the history of your necklace."

"And you could bring me with you?" Maya's heart was racing, on fire. She wanted this so, so badly.

"I think so . . ."

"Oh, yes! Please? Let's try?" Maya was doing her best not to beg, but it was hard.

"Alright. I-I've never brought someone with me, so I'm not exactly sure how to do it, but . . ." She bit her lip and thought for a moment. "If you give me the necklace . . ."

Maya unclasped it and placed it softly into Scarlett's hand.

Scarlett brushed her braid aside with her free hand. "Okay, now . . . put one hand on the necklace and the other on my shoulder. Don't let go." Maya positioned herself.

"Ready?" Scarlett asked.

Maya nodded.

"Let's go."

Scarlett closed her eyes, and the hospital room disappeared, replaced by an inky blackness that stretched forever.

"Is this the right place?" Maya whispered.

"Just wait." As Scarlett spoke, memories flooded around them. They were immersed in a scene. Two people were standing in a jewelry shop: one was a man, tall, with golden hair and green eyes, and the other was a woman, shorter, with brown hair so similar to Maya's and soft brown eyes. The man held up a necklace in his hand. Maya gasped. It was her necklace; it had the same brilliant hue, the same dove on the front. Love pulsed through the air.

"In honor of opening our own jewelry shop, my dear Caroline." The man placed the necklace around the woman's neck. They kissed, and as they did, a beam of light shot through the window, seeming to come from the sky, and hit the necklace, filling it with a glow. "You have our blessing," a voice whispered, but the couple didn't seem to hear it.

Maya looked around the shop in front of her, out of the display windows that faced a cheery street. And then Maya realized it. The street was Harding Street. And the shop . . . 15 Harding Street. Maya almost cried.

Then she and Scarlett were moving forward in time. It was a few years later, it seemed, and the woman, Caroline, sat on the grass in front of a small cottage, surrounded by a white picket fence. The necklace hung around her neck, and she stretched out, patting her slightly swollen tummy. "Oh, my little baby," she murmured.

Another memory. The couple was standing in their jewelry shop at 15 Harding Street. Outside, the street was grey and bleak. Caroline no longer looked pregnant, and she was holding a baby with tufts of brown hair, whose eyes shone with flecks of silver and gold. The baby babbled and reached for the necklace around her mother's neck. "Yeah?" Caroline said to the baby in a sweet voice. "You like Mummy's necklace, Maya?" Her voice was soft and caring, her accent a mix of Cloudian and English. Maya was crying now, tears pouring down her face as she saw her mother call her by name.

"Jonathan?" Caroline said to her husband, who had drifted away to check a bracelet display. "Look at Maya."

Jonathan returned to his wife and daughter, his green eyes full of so much love. He laughed as Maya reached for Caroline's necklace again and again. "You like that, huh? I'll make you a matching one when you're a little older, my sweet. A beautiful necklace for my beautiful girl."

Maya was silent, but she was truly sobbing.

"Do you want to keep going?" Scarlett asked.

Maya nodded vigorously, blinking her tears away, ashamed of being caught crying.

More scenes passed, more time, until Maya saw a scene that she knew all too well. She closed her eyes, for she knew what was going to happen. But she heard the laughs of the family on the lawn, and then she heard the cries as clouds gathered, and figures appeared at the gate. More shouts, and then Maya knew she was in the tunnel, traveling to the Land of the Clouds.

"Ready?" Scarlett whispered.

"Yeah. We can leave now."

And just like that, they returned to the hospital room where Auntie lay.

"Thank you," Maya said, "for showing me that." There was something warm in her chest, a feeling of love that was spreading, a feeling that had always been there, perhaps, but one she had forgotten existed. Her mind was filled with images of her parents, of herself, of their life on Earth.

They were quiet for a few minutes, and then Maya spoke up. "The very first scene, when my dad"—the word was weird to say—"gave my mom"—weird, again—"the necklace, there was a beam of light or something that hit it. And then something said, like, 'we will protect you.' What was that?"

Scarlett shrugged. "I'm not sure. It seemed like the light came—"

"—from the Land of the Clouds." Maya's eyes lit up. "Maybe someone in the Land put some kind of magical protection in the necklace to help my parents, except then they gave it to me, and when I tried to use my power, it helped me . . . It—it boosted it, or something."

"Yeah . . ." Scarlett said. "Maybe. There's a lot of magic in the Land that we don't know about."

"But what is my power?" Maya said. She wanted to get up and pace some more.

"Controlling light? I don't know. I mean, you did control light. And I'd assume that since a bunch of beams of light went through the walls and stuff, you caused all of the OCT all over the world to disappear."

Maya smiled thoughtfully. "That would be pretty cool. But is controlling light a power?"

"It's a rare one. I've never heard anyone having it—"

"Me either . . ."

"—but haven't we been told that rare powers have become even rarer lately? So it would make sense that we didn't really know about it."

"Yeah." There was a pause. "I have so much to ask Auntie when she wakes up."

Scarlett nodded. They lapsed into another awkward silence. After about ten minutes, Scarlett stood up. "I should probably go. But, um, I'll come by again later."

Maya nodded, and Scarlett left.

She sat in silence, staring out the window. She felt all abuzz after seeing her parents. She touched the necklace. It had been magical to see them. And yet . . . something about that trip into the past was making her feel even more unsettled. She had realized something, though she didn't know what, and it was making her squirm again.

What if she had gotten to grow up with her parents? What would've happened then? If she had grown up on Earth, she supposed, she might've felt freer, more at peace. But what about the Land? It was her home—it had to be her home, right?

The journey was over. She had gone to Earth, completed the prophecy. So why were so many things still so confusing? She rubbed her grubby face. She hadn't had the chance—or energy—to wash up yet. The dirt on her face, the few tears in her tunic, they were like battle scars, reminders of her time on Earth. And she wasn't sure that she wanted them to go away yet.

She sighed. She turned to face Auntie, whose eyes were still closed. Maya hoped she would wake up. She had to wake up. Maya needed her . . .

Then, as she watched, something happened. Auntie's eyelids opened, revealing shining blue eyes. Maya gasped in delight, her hand over her mouth. Auntie's gaze swiveled, and at the sight of Maya, she broke into a huge grin. Maya bent over her and hugged her, her eyes shining with happiness, with tears. All their worries were forgotten for the moment as they cried together, united at last.

"I missed you so much," Maya said.

Epilogue

Maya stood by her window, wrapped in a bathrobe, letting the night air wash over her face. A dream had woken her a few minutes ago—*the* dream, in fact. But ever since Scarlett had showed her the memories of her parents, the dream was less scary. She looked forward to it, looked forward to seeing her parents.

She'd tried to fall back asleep afterward, but tonight her mind was racing. It had been three weeks since her return to the Land of the Clouds. So much had happened since then. When Auntie recovered, Maya had told her everything, every detail of her journey on Earth and about what had happened in the OCT headquarters, and the memories Scarlett had revealed to her, and her theory about how the necklace was some sort of amulet. Now Auntie was helping train Maya to use her powers so she could control light, bending it into all sorts of shapes—ropes, spears, and more—without the help of the necklace.

Maya had also told Auntie, after a lot of hesitation, that she had started feeling more and more uncomfortable in the Land of the Clouds, more and more out of place. She told Auntie about how much she'd loved Earth, about how much she missed it. And the memories of her parents, she said, had helped her realize that. Her parents had been happier on Earth, and Maya knew she would be too, knew that she held this connection in common with her parents.

And so, after a lot of thinking, and after consulting with a lot of officials, they had come up with a deal. When Maya turned eighteen, she would move. She would leave the

Land of the Clouds and fulfill her life on Earth. And Maya would be allowed to return to the Land of the Clouds at any time she wished, though she felt that would be infrequently.

She hadn't told Scarlett yet. They hadn't really talked much in the last few weeks anyway. It seemed their friendship had changed. It wasn't gone—they weren't hostile to each other—but it felt like they were being drawn down different paths. Maybe those paths would cross again sometime in the future, Maya thought, but for now, she was fine being acquaintances.

Sometimes she thought of Freddy. Then she would either tear up or rage, depending on her mood. But she missed him, even if he had secretly been von Hopsburg in the end. Occasionally, she remembered the other people she'd met on Earth, like the kids in the orphanage or the two police officers in London, and then she missed Earth particularly.

At those times, and now was one of those times, she would stare outside and think of Earth lying in wait below her, think of clouds and rain and everything else that made Earth special, and smile—for she knew she would see it all again.

ACKNOWLEDGMENTS

First, I would like to thank Emma and everyone else at *Stone Soup*, not only for running the contest that I wrote this novel for but also for finding creative ways to keep kids like myself engaged with writing and reading all throughout the COVID-19 pandemic.

I would also like to thank Richard Geist, my grandfather; Mark Geist, my uncle; and Madeline Nohrnberg, a good friend, for being the first people to read my book cover to cover. Your feedback has been invaluable.

Thanks to Lucy Rados, Isaac and Naomi Shertzer, and all of my friends who listened as I blabbed on and on about my ideas.

Thanks to my whole family, who have inspired me throughout this whole process. And most importantly, thank you, Mom and Dad, for supporting me through every step I take and loving me always.

ABOUT STONE SOUP

Stone Soup is the international literary magazine and website publishing writing and art by young people under the age of 14. Founded in 1973, we have published more creative work by children than any other publisher, selecting the very best from thousands of submissions every year.

Subscribers to *Stone Soup* receive eleven issues of our carefully curated magazine each year (monthly, with a combined summer issue).

Online, subscribers can read the magazine alongside blog posts on a range of subjects from our young bloggers, including book and film reviews, and view multimedia artworks that can't be published in a print format. Our website also features author interviews, contests, educator resources, and more.

Once a year we print the *Stone Soup Annual*, a beautiful full-color book that collates the year's issues alongside the best written work from our blog.

Our book series, *The Stone Soup Books of . . .*, is a growing collection of themed anthologies bringing together some of the finest stories and poems from our archives.

This book is part of a series of long-form work by young authors. It was selected to be published as an "Editor's Choice" from our 2020 Book Contest.

Stone Soup is managed and supported by the Children's Art Foundation, a 501(c)(3) educational charity based in Santa Cruz, California. Join us to support and encourage the writers and artists of the future.

Visit Stonesoup.com to find out more.

OTHER STONE SOUP BOOKS

The Other Realm, a novel by Tristan Hui (14)
The Golden Elephant, poems by Analise Braddock (8)
Three Days Till EOC, a novella by Abhimanyu Sukhdial (12)
Searching for Bow and Arrows, poems by Tatiana Rebecca Shrayer (12)

The Stone Soup Book of Animal Stories
The Stone Soup Book of Family Stories
The Stone Soup Book of Fantasy Stories
The Stone Soup Book of Friendship Stories
The Stone Soup Book of Historical Fiction
The Stone Soup Book of Festival and Holiday Stories
The Stone Soup Book of Poetry
The Stone Soup Book of Science Fiction
The Stone Soup Book of Sports Stories

Stone Soup Annual 2017
Stone Soup Annual 2018
Stone Soup Annual 2019
Stone Soup Annual 2020

CPSIA information can be obtained
at www.ICGtesting.com
Printed in the USA
BVHW062017101121
621198BV00008B/857

9 780894 091155